HEAD START II

English for Cross-cultural Communication

Patricia Che

關於作者

車蓓群

1985 到 2007 年間，身為大學老師的我，藉著各種校內外的課程，有幸接觸到不同程度與不同需求的學習者。在他們身上，我反覆的看到二個現象：第一是無論他們的程度與需求為何，大部分的學習者，都將英語視為一門深奧嚴肅、需要努力研讀與分析的學科，而忘了語言本身存在的目的並不是為了要供人們研讀，而是為了要溝通；也就是說，語言的使用除了有嚴肅的課題外，更有趣味與生活的面向。第二則是語言的學習，常獨立於語言所相互依存的社會文化習俗，及溝通所使用的身體語言之外。

這二個現象讓我很想做一本教科書，是不那麼嚴肅、帶點小趣味，可以直接利用在生活中、但卻直接切中現今社會中十分重要的種種跨文化議題。34 年英語學習與 22 年英語教學的經驗告訴我，即使沒有正經八百或正襟危坐的研讀英語，學習者還是可以開開心心，並且信心十足的使用這個語言來溝通。After all, I did it. I hope you can be just like me: Enjoy English and allow it to be part of your daily life!

國際化、國際化公民、地球村等等,都是這些年喊的震天價響的一些口號,帽子很大,理想很高,但到底要如何落實呢?除了會英文之外,還有沒有別的面向是作為一個國際化公民應該知道的?

我們可以肯定地說:「有!而且還不少!」跨文化、跨族群的溝通牽涉到的不只是語言,更是對其他人的尊重、對社會議題的了解、對環境的愛護,以及同理心的建立—這是最重要的。只有對以上這些面向都有所了解並努力實踐後,人與人之間才能產生有效率且沒有誤解的溝通。

本套教材就是依照這樣的理念,在第一冊時將跨文化溝通與較基本的身體語言的學習,藉由自美國來台灣工作的一家人帶出,架構在聽說讀寫的基本技巧上,利用吃、喝、玩、樂、工作及生活的各種場景來反覆練習有效的溝通。而在第二冊,我們則更進一步地讓這一家人面對生活中更高層次的問題與挑戰,同樣架構在英文的聽說讀寫技能訓練上,讓讀者能於感同身受之餘,同時學習一些可立即使用的字詞和句子。

因此,本書中每一個課次都以社會中某一個面向為主題,如師生關係、約會習俗、同性戀、樂活族 (LOHAS) 及蘇活族 (SOHO) 等,以聽、說、讀、寫的方式進行內容的介紹。每一個主題常使用的關鍵字詞會先以圖片來介紹,接著將這些圖片中的字詞放在對話和接下來的聽力練習中。反覆之後,會有引導式口說練習,將前面介紹的字詞直接放進不同場景的對話中，去嘗試真正使用它們。接著我們將與主題相關的跨文化溝通知識以短文方式呈現，並佐以閱讀測驗練習。另外，依據大量閱讀的重要性及跨文化、跨族群議題的多面向，我們還安排了每課兩篇延伸閱讀來分享更多知識。下一個單元則是有系統地介紹在寫作中，學習者最常碰到的一些文法與段落鋪陳問題，如單複數與冠詞的用法、因果關係與對比的敘述等。這單元是以 1、3、5、7 課次介紹新的議題，2、4、6、8 課次延伸前一課之議題的方式來進行。同時為了讓學習的成效更為明顯，我們還針對每個主題另闢符合英檢題型的 TEST ZONE，讓讀者可以隨時挑戰自己對這個主題的理解。

我們衷心希望能利用這些社會中越來越為大家所接受並廣泛討論的主題，以反覆練習的架構，讓所有讀者能在英文進步的同時，對跨文化與跨族群溝通的各種議題有多一層的了解，進而建立對不同文化與族群的人的同理心，而最終能成為真正的國際化公民。

車蓓群 謹識

本書使用指南

WHERE IT ALL BEGINS

＊在本單元中，你將學到：

一個廣受社會討論、具有爭議性，卻又與生活
息息相關的議題。此議題的核心概念以清楚的
跨頁大圖呈現，並列出與此議題相關的關鍵
字詞。

＊因此，你應該要：

先試著用自己的意思解說大圖，然後學習
列出的關鍵字詞；最後，利用所學字詞再重
新詮釋一次大圖，讓自己確實掌握這些字詞代表的意義。

CONVERSATION

＊在本單元中，你將學到：

真實發生在你我身邊的對話內容。此單元讓你與書中人物一起面對
該議題可能引起的現實狀況，確實達到真正「角色扮演」(role play)
的目的，進而自然地以英語表達對各式議題的意見或觀感。

＊因此，你應該要：

先理解對話中人物面對該狀況的態度以及之後採取的作法，然後進
行模擬對話練習。切記要確實模仿這些人物的語氣、音調，以及可能會出現的表情。對話之後
的聽力和口說練習可讓你更熟悉英語對話的模式。

CORE READING +
EXTENDED READING

＊在本單元中，你將學到：

本書的核心部分─經由精細的閱讀過程，了解
該議題所涵蓋的不同因素、角度及立場。目標
是要讓你對於議題產生深入的思索(thinking)，
而不只是擷取資訊(information)。

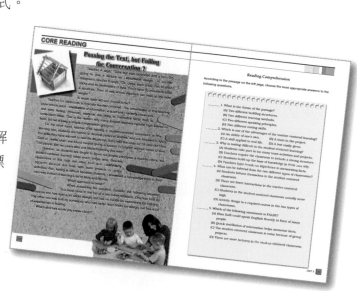

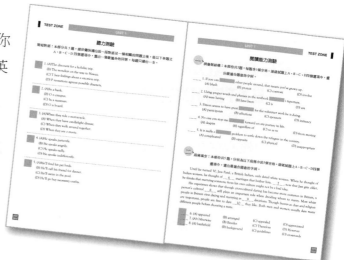

＊因此，你應該要：

　　先試著自己閱讀文章，並且確實作答閱讀測驗，然後才藉由生字表或工具書的幫助，檢核自己的理解程度。務必徹底了解該主題與各篇文章，努力讓自己用「純」英語產生個人見解。

WRITING CORNER

＊在本單元中，你將學到：

　　新穎、不同於一般教條式的作文概念。此單元著重在「從架構中學習，從錯誤中加強」的寫作方式，其中該單元的習題是不可錯過的鍛鍊利器。

＊因此，你應該要：

　　快速並確實掌握寫作的內容重點，接著在習題部分認真分析範文，讓自己有清楚的大綱概念。另一方面，文法部分以特殊的「改錯」方式為學習主軸，引導你從錯誤中反思，並且學到真正實用且重要的文法基本功。

TEST ZONE

＊在本單元中，你將學到：

　　與全民英檢考試結合的各類題型。此單元讓你有效地複習課本內容，同時讓你有機會模擬英檢考試。

＊因此，你應該要：

　　每學習完一個完整課次，就給自己小小的挑戰，完成聽、讀、寫三種英檢題型。其中，翻譯題和寫作的題目都是精心配合每課的主題，是相當重要的成果驗收。

Contents

Scope and Sequence

Unit	WHERE IT ALL BEGINS	CONVERSATION	CORE READING
1	"Would you like to go out with me?""Sure!"	Dating Customs	Dating My Way, or Yours?
2	"My father is cooking and cleaning the house. How about yours?"	Gender Role Play	Women Get Tough
3	"You can advance work from anywhere!"	SOHO Working	SOHO Success
4	"We can only be famous for 15 minutes."	The Paparazzi Phenomenon	The Paparazzi Profiles
5	"Mr. Rogan, let's do Unit Five today."	Teacher-student Relations	Passing the Test, but Failing the Conversation?
6	"We are all made of flesh and blood. It shouldn't matter what sex you choose to love."	Gay Issues	Gay at Great Risk
7	"Let's live in LOHAS!"	Trends of LOHAS	Living in LOHAS
8	"Without heart, there can be no understanding among us all."	Politically Correct English	To Be PC or Not to Be PC?

Acknowledgements

All articles in this publication are adapted from the works by:

Amelia Smolar, Doug Hinnant, Jamie Blackler, Jason Crockett, Joe Chan, M. J. McAteer, Junnita Gustafson, and Paul Geraghty.

Photo Credits

All pictures in this publication are authorized for use by:

Dearmstime, iStockphoto, and ShutterStock.

Meet the Parkers

The Parkers have just moved from the U.S. to Taiwan.

"Would you like to go out with me?" "Sure!"

1. on a date 約會（中）
2. chaperone n. （社交場合出現的）監督者
3. dating coach 約會教練
4. body language 肢體語言
5. eye contact 眼光接觸
6. surveillance n. 監控
7. ice-breaker 開場白
8. gift n. 禮物

CONVERSATION I

🎧(2) **Chris (C) is walking around, and his good friend, William (W), is standing beside.**

W: *Give me a break, Chris! You've been* [1] ***strolling*** *back and forth all around. What's up?*

C: *I can't help it! I'll have the first date with a girl I like tomorrow. I get nervous.*

W: *Not to worry. You just need some good tips for dating. Here's your super dating coach...ME!*

C: *Dating coach? You mean I need you to be my coach for dating? You must be kidding!*

W: *Why not? You need an experienced coach for playing sports, right? Why not for dating?*

C: *Mm.... I've got to say you have your point. Ok, now, let's see how much you can coach me.*

W: *Okay,* [2] ***first off***, *you must make a good impression, so you need to act confidently, and you have to watch all the gestures and body languages you make. Also, never be late.*

C: *Wow, sounds quite professional. Okay, go on.*

W: *Okay, you should take a shower and shave yourself clean. You know, no women like to date a* [3] ***sloppy*** *man. By the way, you need to come up with interesting topics for conversation at dinner, on a walk, or in whatever situation.*

C: *I can't believe how much I should prepare for the date! Hey, coach, keep on giving me more advice, okay?*

W: *No problem. The service fee per hour is NT$2,000 for* [4] ***one-on-one*** *coaching. If you prefer coaching* [5] ***in company***, *I'll charge a little bit more.*

C: *What? You mean you're going to charge me for all the advice you've given?*

W: *Don't worry. I'm your good friend, and I'll charge you for only NT$500 an hour.*

C: *You* [6] ***sly*** *guy!*

Words and Phrases

1. stroll [strol] *v.* 漫步
2. first off　(口語)首先
3. sloppy [slɑpɪ] *adj.* 邋遢的
4. one-on-one [ˋwʌnɑnˋwʌn] *adj.* 一對一的
5. in company　一起，結伴
6. sly [slaɪ] *adj.* 狡猾的

Listening Practice

Listen to the following questions or statements, and choose the most appropriate responses.

_____ 1. (A) He is upstairs waiting for you.
  (B) I've failed in the test.
  (C) The view is so wonderful.
  (D) What are you eating now?

_____ 2. (A) I'll fix the problem for you.
  (B) I will see you later.
  (C) Got it, and I'll be on time then.
  (D) Did we meet before?

_____ 3. (A) Yeah, I just bought a new couch.
  (B) There are ten coaches on the train.
  (C) Nope, where should I get it?
  (D) Well, she looks quite professional.

_____ 4. (A) Hope you'll do it well.
  (B) Thank you for preparing the food for me.
  (C) It's a wonderful view.
  (D) Tomorrow will be a fine day.

_____ 5. (A) I believe I can get somewhere.
  (B) He seems to be curious.
  (C) Sorry, I just can't help it.
  (D) Our nerve system is complicated.

CONVERSATION II

🎧 **Chris (C) is sitting at his desk, and William (W) is coming into the classroom.**

W: Hey, ¹***buddy***, you're here. How's your ²***fantastic*** dating?

C: Oh, forget about it! It was a total mess!

W: How come? Didn't you use all the tips I gave you?

C: Yeah, I tried to, but guess what? You didn't coach me to keep away from any ³***date crashers***!

W: What date-crashers?

C: You won't believe this—the girl's mom and dad came on our date!

W: Her mom and dad? What did they show up there for?

C: Who knows? It was terrible anyway. They kept following and watching us all the way, even in the convenience store!

W: Seems like they're afraid you're going to eat her or something like that.

C: You bet. Even when I ⁴***leaned*** near to listen to her, her father shouted, "Don't let him touch you!" Come on, it was in the park, and everybody there was laughing!

W: Oh, boy, sounds like a big ⁵***disaster***.

C: Yeah, I really ⁶***lost face***, ⁷***blushing*** all the way, especially when her mom and dad kept looking at me all over with ⁸***distrust***! What's the problem with their mind?

W: Maybe next time you can bring your parents with you on your date as well.

C: What? Bring my parents? Well, what are they supposed to do?

W: Ha, I believe parents on both sides will have a good time discussing your bright future.

C: Hey, stop teasing me, okay?

Words and Phrases

1. buddy [ˋbʌdɪ] *n.* (口語)老兄；朋友
2. fantastic [fænˋtæstɪk] *adj.* 很棒的
3. date crasher   約會不請自來的不速之客
4. lean [lin] *v.* 傾斜，屈身
5. disaster [dɪˋzæstɚ] *n.* 災難
6. lose face   丟臉
7. blush [blʌʃ] *v.* 臉紅
8. distrust [dɪsˋtrʌst] *n.* 不信任

Oral Practice

Part I: Blank-filling dialogues

❶ A: Hey, buddy, you're here. How's your conference? It must be ▨▨▨▨▨▨▨.

B: Oh, ▨▨▨▨▨▨▨▨▨▨ it! It was ▨▨▨▨▨▨▨▨▨▨!

A: ▨▨▨▨▨▨▨▨▨▨? Didn't you use all the ▨▨▨▨▨▨ I gave you?

B: Yeah, I tried to, but ▨▨▨▨▨▨▨▨▨? You didn't teach me to test the microphone and stereo first.

❷ A: Oh, dear, sounds like your interview was a big ▨▨▨▨▨▨.

B: Yeah, I really ▨▨▨▨▨▨▨▨, blushing all the way, especially when one of the interviewers ▨▨▨▨▨▨▨▨▨ at me all over with a funny look! What's the ▨▨▨▨▨▨▨▨ with their mind?

A: Maybe ▨▨▨▨▨▨▨▨ you should give them the funny look ▨▨▨▨▨ ▨▨▨▨▨.

B: Hey, stop ▨▨▨▨▨▨ me, okay?

Part II: Open discussions

❶ Have you ever had a good date? What do you think makes a good date?

❷ To your mind, what should an ideal date probably look like?

Dating My Way, or Yours?

A tall, dark, handsome American man is looking at his date, a big-eyed Indian girl with a beautiful smile. They have been dating a few times, and everything seems to go well. All his friends suppose they are going to be a ¹**fabulous** couple. He himself is also thinking, "Boy, with this pretty young woman, I bet I can live happily ever after."

Can that be true? It is probably not.

From culture to culture, dating customs are greatly different, making it difficult for people from different backgrounds to meet.

In general, westerners are more liberal in dating than the rest of the world. This is especially true in the United States and the United Kingdom, where ²**online** dating has been common. ³**In contrast**, the Japanese prefer to meet people by means of close friends and they are not used to searching for possible mates on the Internet.

Culture factors also determine the ⁴**pace** at which a ⁵**romance** can progress. In the United States and in Germany, ⁶**physical** ⁷**intimacy**, such as holding hands and kissing, is normal at the early stage in a relationship. In ⁸**Korea**, on the other hand, kissing is not considered proper for those only on a few dates.

Also, parents may pressure their sons and daughters to date someone within their own culture. Indian family members, for example, usually live together closely, so any ⁹**outsider** may feel ¹⁰**uneasy** or uncomfortable in the big family. Therefore, our tall, dark, handsome American gentleman will have a better chance to live happily ever after with the Indian girl, only if he is able to live with her "whole" family.

Even if cultural differences may make dating difficult and ¹¹**complicated**, with understanding and patience, forming a close ¹²**bond** with someone from a different culture opens minds and ¹³**softens** hearts.

▶ *see WORD BANK FOR READINGS page 156*

Reading Comprehension

According to the passage on the left page, choose the most appropriate answers to the following questions.

_____ 1. What is the main idea in the passage?

(A) Dating may cost much money and take much time.

(B) Everybody should have various dates all over the world.

(C) It is better not to try to date someone from another culture.

(D) Dating can be complicated due to cultural differences.

_____ 2. In which country can people be viewed as conservative in dating?

(A) The United States.　　　　(B) Korea.

(C) The United Kingdom.　　　(D) Germany.

_____ 3. Which may NOT be one of the vital factors mentioned that might affect a date?

(A) The weather on that day.

(B) The attitudes of the family.

(C) The pace that a romance progresses.

(D) Understanding of cultural differences.

_____ 4. Which is the latest form for people in the world to have a date?

(A) Meeting each other in the park.

(B) Holding each other's hands.

(C) Contacting each other online.

(D) Knowing each other via close friends.

_____ 5. Which of the following statements is TRUE?

(A) Dating is not only a love issue but a cultural lesson.

(B) People in the United Kingdom dare not meet possible mates online.

(C) It is cheaper to have a close bond with someone in another culture.

(D) Very often, Asian people are the most open in dating.

🎧⁶ Chaperones Are Watching

Oh, love. A beautiful, young couple walks hand-in-hand through a quiet park with flowers ¹**blooming** around. Now they are resting on the bench where they are ²**gazing** at each other with ³**affection**. The girl closes her eyes as her date leans towards her for her kiss....

Suddenly, a large hand covers the boy's face and pushes him away, and the girl's aunt sits down in the tiny space between them and crosses her arms.

Here enters the chaperone!

A "chaperone," or a "chaperon," is ⁴**referred** to an adult who watches over young, unmarried people in social meetings. A chaperone's responsibility is to make sure that the young people will not do anything ⁵**illegal** or ⁶**inappropriate**. The title is also used for teachers and parents who help ⁷**supervise** social events such as school parties or dance balls.

The word "chaperone" comes from the French word "chaperon," which means "⁸**hood**." It is believed that the meaning comes from the hoods used to cover hunting ⁹**falcons'** heads so that they would not fly away. Therefore, when the word is used in dating, it possibly means parents want to protect daughters from "flying away" with their dates.

In earlier days, chaperones were older, married women who ¹⁰**accompanied** a young woman to places where young men were present, in order to protect the ¹¹**virtue** of the young lady they watched over.

One popular example of chaperones was shown in the movie *The* ¹²***Godfather***. The main character, Michael Corleone, fell in love with a young woman named Apollonia in Italy. When Michael went dating with Apollonia, her whole family followed them, staying a few feet behind the couple. Apollonia's whole family was acting as a chaperone to make sure that she stayed safe with Michael.

Most of the young people nowadays cannot imagine being watched over while dating. However, it can be said that, instead of ¹³**ruining** their fun, chaperones are there to protect them from doing anything they may regret later.

▶ *see WORD BANK FOR READINGS page 156*

Reading Comprehension

According to the passage on the left page, choose the most appropriate answers to the following questions.

_____ 1. What is the theme of the passage?

    (A) A discussion over a role adults play in young people's dating.

    (B) A discovery of hunters and their hunting tools.

    (C) A description of a classic movie about a big Italian family.

    (D) A diary of a beautiful young couple happy together.

_____ 2. Which is NOT related to the word "chaperone" in its meaning?

    (A) Chaperon.   (B) Hood.   (C) Shelter.   (D) Protector.

_____ 3. Which is NOT one of the duties a chaperone would do?

    (A) Watching over young people on their dates.

    (B) Offering useful tips on report writing.

    (C) Supervising social events like parties or balls.

    (D) Protecting the virtue of young unmarried people.

_____ 4. Which of the following statements is TRUE?

    (A) It would be a chaperone's mission to make a date romantic.

    (B) Chaperone originally means hunters looking for animals.

    (C) A chaperone would allow young people to smoke or drink.

    (D) Most teens nowadays may view it as strange to be watched over on a date.

_____ 5. What can be inferred about the author's thinking on chaperones?

    (A) They just play their roles on marvelous stages.

    (B) They just live their life in ridiculous ways.

    (C) They just show their authority with cruel means.

    (D) They just do their duties out of good will.

On Your Mark, Get Set, Date!

Time to begin!

You only had three minutes to impress the woman in your face. You were sweating to find some proper words to speak out, but too nervous to [1]**utter** anything. After an [2]**awkward** 30-second silence, the woman [3]**impatiently** checked her watch, asking, "Isn't time up?" You blushed, knowing you've failed again....

Welcome to the world of "speed dating," which serves a way to meet your possible date "much" more quickly.

Speed dating now has become one of the hottest means for finding a partner in Japan.

Generally, about 20 men and the equal number of women pay a fee to meet one another. [4]**Participants** are separately given ID tags and [5]**scorecards**. Fixed seats are [6]**assigned** to the females. Then, the men have to [7]**rotate** through seats, sitting opposite the women for a timed date of only two to five minutes.

After every short meeting, participants need to mark "yes" or "no" on each of their scorecards to answer key questions like, "Would you like to see this person again?" When two people say yes to one another, the dating service will put them in further contact later on.

Speed dating is advertised as an efficient means for busy singles to find true love. "I don't have a girlfriend. It's difficult to meet good women at work. That's why I'm here," said one office worker in [8]**Tokyo**, echoing a common problem among singles in Japan.

The Japanese government even [9]**sponsors** speed dating to keep the country [10]**populated**. According to the statistics, Japan has one of the world's lowest birth rates—1.28 children per woman.

However, there is as much [11]**embarrassment** as romance in speed dating. One woman was asked, "What do you do for fun when you are all alone?" Though thinking it was too personal, she tried to answer, "I sleep."

Of course, compared with hours of pain involved in a traditional blind date, a few minutes of [12]**discomfort** seem to be nothing. After all, time is too short to be upset about one date gone bad, as there are 19 more along the line.

> *see WORD BANK FOR READINGS page 156*

Reading Comprehension

According to the passage on the left page, choose the most appropriate answers to the following questions.

_____ 1. What is the main issue discussed in the passage?
   (A) A memorable romance.
   (B) A leisure TV program.
   (C) An efficient dating method.
   (D) A game show.

_____ 2. Which is NOT one of the activities usually seen in speed dating?
   (A) Participants mark "yes" or "no" on each of their scoreboards.
   (B) The host provides a fabulous entertainment in advance.
   (C) Participants rotate to meet each other in a short time.
   (D) The host gives participants ID tags individually.

_____ 3. Now in Japan, how does speed dating seem?
   (A) It is one of the hottest issues in Japanese society.
   (B) It is no longer popular in Japan.
   (C) It is advertised as a scary means for busy singles to find love.
   (D) There is no sponsor from the Japanese government.

_____ 4. What does the author imply in the last paragraph?
   (A) Speed dating is a less embarrassing way of meeting people than traditional blind date.
   (B) There are too few participants in speed dating.
   (C) Speed dating should be totally free of charge.
   (D) Officials in the government should do more speed dating.

_____ 5. Which of the following statements is FALSE?
   (A) Birth rate in Japan is low.
   (B) Embarrassment may come along in speed dating.
   (C) The speed dating service help people further contact in pairs.
   (D) Japanese always take time dating various people.

Providing Examples: Part I
提供例證（一）

1. 提供例證是寫作時說明論點最常使用的方法。

2. 使用提供例證的方式可讓抽象概念(abstract notion)獲得具體解釋(concrete explanation)，而使讀者藉由實際例子了解討論中的觀點。

3. 在使用提供例證的方法來發展段落時，可用幾個簡短的例子解釋一個主要概念。在某些狀況下，也可能只用一個例子，但相對的必須提出足夠的細節說明。

4. 提供例證時，最重要的準則就是例子必須要適當、具體並且清楚。

Drills: In each of the following paragraphs, separately mark out its main idea and supporting examples.

1. Indian family members are close and often live together, so any outsider may feel uneasy or uncomfortable in the big family. That is, an American who marries an Indian girl may find it difficult to live with his wife's whole family, because he has to communicate with everybody there.

2. Speed dating is advertised as an efficient way for busy singles to find their love. Echoing the common problem, one office worker in Tokyo said, "I don't have a girlfriend, and it's difficult to meet good women at work. That's why I'm here."

3. There are various ways to show a feeling of love. Many Europeans are used to kissing and hugging. Some tribes in the North Pole keep their noses touching among one another. Some aborigines in South Africa even express their happiness by crying loudly.

4. Water is indispensable. First off, water serves as a surviving element for all living creatures. The crew on a ship takes water as a path of course. A farmer would harvest no crops if there was insufficient water. A firefighter use water as a sharp weapon to put off a fire. Water has even become a vital source for electricity in the power plant.

WRITING CORNER : GRAMMAR

Avoiding Improper Use of Pronoun: Part I
避免不當使用代名詞（一）

1. 具有代替名詞功能的字詞稱為代名詞(pronoun)。
2. 使用代名詞是為了方便代稱重複提到的名詞。最常使用的代名詞為人稱代名詞 (personal pronouns)，包括：I, you, he, she, it, we, they，以及所衍生的所有格(my, your, his, her, its, our, their)和受格(me, you, him, her, it, us, them) 等。
3. 使用代名詞時，應站在讀者的角度出發，檢查所使用的代名詞是否清楚明瞭，讓讀者能夠輕易分辨。如果使用的代名詞不夠清楚，就有必要重新寫成原來要代稱的名詞，或是調整字句的順序，直到句意夠清楚為止。
4. 代名詞在文章裡距離所代稱的名詞太遠時，就有必要使用名詞，避免讀者混淆或困惑。尤其在介紹專有名詞時，可以不用太擔心重複名詞，造成過度使用代名詞。

Drills: In both of the following paragraphs, find out improper uses of personal pronouns, and correct them into appropriate forms.

1. Chaperones are adults who watch over young, unmarried people in social meetings. Their responsibility is to prevent them from doing anything impolite or illegal. In earlier days, they were older, married women who accompanied them to meet each other to protect the traditional virtue. Nowadays, most of them may not imagine being watched over while dating out. However, they are there to protect them from doing something they may regret later.

2. Trans fat is an important material used to preserve food, so almost every food contains it in the States, and Americans take in large amounts of it in a year. It is very often found in baked food, and it has been largely used for deep frying. However, recently, it has been reported to have an ill impact on human body in the long term. Hence, it is now under discussion that if its use should be restricted, or if it should be banned from being used in food.

🎧⁹ "My father is cooking and cleaning the house. How about yours?"

❶ paternity leave 父親育嬰假	❹ gender-specific *adj.* 因性別而特定的	❼ gender concern 性別考量
❷ maternity leave 母親育嬰假	❺ coeducational *adj.* 男女合校的	❽ competence *n.* 能力
❸ child care and education 孩子養育和教育	❻ decision-maker *n.* 決策者	

CONVERSATION I

🎧 **Laura (L) is at her office, and her colleague, Helen (H), is talking with her.**

L : *Helen, what's going on? You've been looking upset these few days.*

H : *Well, Laura, to be honest, I'm afraid that I have to hand in a* [1]***resignation*** *notice.*

L : *A resignation notice? Wait a minute, Helen. We know you've been performing well in your position. And, you're so* [2]***enthusiastic*** *about your job. So, what happened actually?*

H : *All right. Laura, you're my good friend, so I should let you know I am choosing to leave just because I have a much higher salary than my husband.*

L : *What? You mean your husband can't accept it, so he asked you to quit?*

H : *Not really. In fact, my husband doesn't care about it at all. But, my* [3]***parents-in-law*** *and the other family members think it's not* [4]***appropriate*** *for a husband to earn less money than his wife.*

L : *But that doesn't* [5]***make sense***, *does it? The money you earn is from your competence!*

H : *Well, Laura, in Taiwan, a wife is still supposed to be in lower status than her husband in almost every way, no matter how competent or highly-educated she may be.*

L : *I know that. But, Helen, for your own sake, don't you ever think you can resist such an* [6]***outdated***, *unreasonable thought?*

H : *Believe me, Laura. I've been struggling, but I REALLY got* [7]***exhausted*** *this time.*

L : *All right, Helen. I think I have to respect your decision.*

H : *Thank you, Laura. You're really a good manager, and a nice friend.*

L : *Well, what can I say? Promise me you'll take care of yourself, okay?*

H : *You too. Thank you for understanding.*

Words and Phrases

1. resignation [ˌrɛzɪgˈneʃən] *n.* 辭職
2. enthusiastic [ɪnˌθjuzɪˈæstɪk] *adj.* 具有熱忱的
3. parents-in-law [ˈpɛrəntsɪnˌlɔ] *n.* 公婆，岳父母
4. appropriate [əˈproprɪɪt] *adj.* 適當的
5. make sense　(事情)有意義
6. outdated [ˌaʊtˈdetɪd] *adj.* 過時的
7. exhausted [ɪgˈzɔstɪd] *adj.* 精疲力盡的

Listening Practice

Listen to the following question or statements, and choose the most appropriate responses.

1. (A) Nothing interesting in particular.
   (B) Yes, the party soon will be starting.
   (C) Every party has its policy.
   (D) We're looking for a place for parking.

2. (A) Well, she looks the other way.
   (B) Anyone can have different looks.
   (C) We need good health care.
   (D) Yeah, he always tries to be neat and clean.

3. (A) No, she usually has the sixth sense.
   (B) Maybe she doesn't want to tell the truth.
   (C) Yes, that's quite sensational.
   (D) I can't see why she's so sensitive.

4. (A) He is an exhausted worker.
   (B) We're heading down the road.
   (C) Have you seen today's newspaper?
   (D) How about having some refreshment?

5. (A) The suitcase can't be placed upside down.
   (B) Let's turn up the radio.
   (C) Yes, I've been informed of the news.
   (D) Patients often feel down in the hospital.

CONVERSATION II

🎧 Henry (H) is [1] **browsing through** [2]**drafts** in the publishing company he works with, and its [3]**editor in chief**, Todd (T), is coming up.

T : Hi, Henry. Good to see you.... Ur.... May I ask what you're wearing?

H : Hi, Todd. Well, this? This is my apron. I was cooking dinner, and we had no tomatoes and carrots. So I went outside to do some shopping, and I came by to take my drafts.

T : Yeah, yeah, I can tell. It was easy to see the huge grocery bag in your hand, and, ur, the bunches of vegetables you bought, even when I was standing far away.

H : Todd, is there anything wrong? To be frank, you're giving a little bit of a [4]**bizarre** look.

T : Well, Henry, sorry to be that straight. But don't you feel VERY awkward for a man to wear an apron like this? And, why is it you, not Laura, that cooks dinner?

H : Awkward how? Wearing no apron when cooking is like wearing no [5]**goggles** when swimming, isn't it? And of course, it's always I that do the cooking, as I'm staying home all day long!

T : I don't know. Still many people suppose a man should be [6]**macho**, so a man in an apron doesn't seem to be, you know, a REAL man. And, isn't cooking an easy duty that a woman should do?

H : Well, Todd, I can't agree to that. I don't understand why cooking has something to do with [7]**masculinity**. And, each family member should do his or her best part to [8]**contribute** to the home.

T : All right, all right. I'm a [9]**conservative**, [10]**old-fashioned** man anyway. I DEFINITELY won't do any cooking, wear an apron, and, ur, ur, carry a grocery bag in my whole life.

H : Okay, you have your point. But what a pity! Being a well-qualified cooking husband brings not only fun but achievement!

Words and Phrases

1. browse [brauz] *v.* 瀏覽
2. draft [dræft] *n.* 草稿；稿子
3. editor in chief　主編
4. bizarre [bɪˋzɑr] *adj.* 奇怪的，異樣的
5. goggles [ˋgɑglz] *n.* (pl.) 蛙鏡
6. macho [ˋmɑtʃo] *adj.* 具男子氣概的
7. masculinity [͵mæskjəˋlɪnətɪ] *n.* 男子氣概
8. contribute [kənˋtrɪbjut] *v.* 貢獻
9. conservative [kənˋsɝvətɪv] *adj.* 保守的
10. old-fashioned [ˋoldˋfæʃənd] *adj.* 老式作風的

Oral Practice

Part I: Blank-filling dialogues

❶ A: Lotus, is there anything wrong? _____, you're giving me a _____ look.

B: Lynn, sorry to be that _____. But, don't you feel it's VERY _____ for a woman to ride a heavy motorbike like this? And, why is it you, not Raymond, that repairs the window?

A: _____. Riding a heavy motorbike is no big deal to me. And, _____, it's I that do the window repairing, as I can't wait for Raymond to do that!

❷ A: Still many people _____ a boss should be serious, so a boss who brews tea for employees _____, you know, a REAL boss. Isn't brewing tea _____ that any employee can do?

B: Well, Marina, I can't _____ that. I don't _____ why brewing tea _____ authority. And, each _____ in the office should _____ the company in anyway he or she can.

Part II: Open discussions

❶ Compare different role expectations of females and males now and then.

❷ If you could make a choice, would you choose to be the same sex you're now, or otherwise? Why?

 ⌂₁₃ Women Get Tough¹

A husband, standing by the door, holds a baby tight. His wife, an army soldier, is going to war. He slowly waves his hand to his wife, whispering goodbye. The ²**armed** wife looks at her dear husband, saying, "Take care of our baby. I will return in no time...."

Wait, Wait! When do women need to fight at war?

For thousands of years, women have played no key roles at war. Fighting in the ³**battlefield** has been considered a basic duty and right for males. It has been thought that, when men go off to fight, women only stay behind in tears, hoping their husbands, sons, or brothers will survive.

However, things have changed. More women have been performing different missions once reserved for men. In contrast, more men have been acting various parts once regarded as female-only. In no area can such the change be more obvious than that in the military.

It is common now for women to participate in the military forces of many countries, such as Taiwan and the United States. In Taiwan, females were permitted to serve in the army starting in 1991. Since then, the number of women joining the military has continued growing. In 2002, a female military officer was promoted as a general for the first time in Taiwan.

Today, there have been over 8,000 female officers in the military of Taiwan, around 7% of the total. Comparing the rate of female ⁴**participation** in the military with that of other countries, Taiwan ranked No. 1 with Japan in ⁵**Asia**.

Even compared with non-Asian countries, Taiwan still stands in a ⁶**leading** ⁷**status**. There are only three countries of NATO with more female military members than those of Taiwan. One example is the United Kingdom, with around 9% of female members in the military.

In the future, female members in the military forces around the world will probably keep increasing. Next time you see a husband waving goodbye to his soldier wife at the door, never be that surprised. After all, women have been getting tough over these years.

> ▷ *see WORD BANK FOR READINGS page 156*

Reading Comprehension

According to the passage on the left page, choose the most appropriate answers to the following questions.

_____ 1. What is the main idea of the passage?

(A) Women have largely showed strengths in the running field.

(B) Women have felt pity to the homeless on the streets.

(C) Women have more and more influence on the military system.

(D) Women have happily got chances to win in the working places.

_____ 2. What does the sentence "When do women need to fight at war" imply?

(A) Serving in the army is still not viewed as normal for women.

(B) Many wars have much to do with women.

(C) Women does not need wars to keep themselves alive.

(D) Surviving the war is important for women.

_____ 3. Which is NOT one of the role changes of females in the military forces?

(A) They have been performing different missions.

(B) They have been searching for partners for life.

(C) They have been participating in more activities.

(D) They have been serving in important positions.

_____ 4. How does the author think of female participation in the military service?

(A) It is an international competition among different countries.

(B) It is a serious marriage issue between various couples.

(C) It is a difficult social problem that bothers many governments.

(D) It is a trend as women have been forceful in these years.

_____ 5. Which of the following statements is TRUE?

(A) For years, fighting at war has not been a right but a duty for women.

(B) Even today, there is still no female ever promoted as a general in history.

(C) Taiwan has the highest rate of female service in the army.

(D) Changes of female role play can be best observed in the military.

My Nights with Elsa

I haven't had a full night of sleep in the last three months. I go to bed for a few hours and wake up in the early morning when every other house on my street is quiet. The reason for my strange habit is my daughter, Elsa. New babies rarely sleep through the night. Since Elsa was born three months ago, I've been waking up every night with her.

Are you wondering where my wife is during my nights with Elsa? My wife is asleep. She has to go to work the next day. In [1]**Norway**, parents have the right to decide how to divide up their time off after their child is born. Our country gives new parents up to 54 weeks of paid time off as a family. Though fathers are given up to six weeks, they can also use part of the total 54 weeks off.

My wife and I were able to choose how to spend our time off with Elsa. Right now she's happy to be back at work and I'm enjoying getting to know my little daughter.

[2]**Parental** leave rules are very different in other countries. While most governments offer a lot of time to mothers, new fathers are not always so lucky. In [3]**Portugal** and Spain, mothers have between 16 and 20 weeks, while fathers have only three weeks.

In [4]**Guatemala**, a mother has twelve weeks with her new baby and a father has only two days. China offers new mothers up to 90 days of paid leave, but has no policy for fathers. In the United States, neither mothers nor fathers get paid time off to spend with their child.

I have friends who would not take the amount of time off that I'm taking. Many men still believe that it's a woman's job to stay home and raise a new child, but I think that idea is outdated. Both parents should get to know their new baby. I wouldn't trade my [5]**sleepless** nights with Elsa for anything.

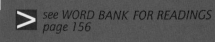

> *see WORD BANK FOR READINGS*
> *page 156*

34

Reading Comprehension

According to the passage on the left page, choose the most appropriate answers to the following questions.

_____ 1. What is the theme of the passage?

(A) A speech from a mother of a missing child.

(B) A confession from a man in prison.

(C) A statement from a lawyer of a big company.

(D) A narration from a father of a newborn baby.

_____ 2. Which country offers the most days off for new parents in total?

(A) The United States.　　　　(B) Norway.

(C) Guatemala.　　　　　　　(D) Portugal.

_____ 3. Why does the father choose to take the days off with his daughter?

(A) He wants to spend more time getting to know her as a new baby.

(B) His wife is unwilling to share the work to take care of their daughter.

(C) The government orders him that he stay home and not work anymore.

(D) His friends would not take the same leave and transfer it to him.

_____ 4. What does the description of the narrator together with his daughter imply?

(A) Living in the quiet neighborhood is helpful to the baby's sleep.

(B) Waking up every night does more or less injury to health.

(C) Taking care of his baby daughter is bittersweet at heart.

(D) Lacking enough rest makes him feel like aging fast.

_____ 5. Which of the following statements is TRUE?

(A) The baby's mother is out of work now, so she is by the baby's side as well.

(B) In Norway, each of the parents has 54 weeks off with their new child.

(C) The narrator seems to be pleased to take parental leave.

(D) In China, it is not mothers but fathers that can take parental leave.

🎧 Who's the Boss Now?

Queen Elizabeth I

Joan of Arc

As the [1]**fearless** [2]**Viking** King is set to sail off, he looks out across the sea, wondering if his wife is doing her duty at home. After all, the world is [3]**dominated** by males, so it is men's job to provide leadership while their women have to support them behind....

[4]**Nevertheless**, for centuries, there have been [5]**numerous** excellent females shining to make a great difference in their times rather than yield to the long-term trend of male domination.

One of the most [6]**inspirational** women in history was Queen Elizabeth I of England. During her rule, Queen Elizabeth guided the country through challenges and difficulties. In the end, she made England one of the greatest [7]**superpowers** on earth.

Joan of Arc was another significant female leader in the past. She was then a teenager, but she led the army to [8]**confront** their [9]**British** enemy, and finally freed her country. Years after her death, she was named a [10]**Saint** by the church for her [11]**contribution** to France.

In modern times, there are far more female leaders than ever before. In 1990, Mary Robinson became the first woman to be elected as President of [12]**Ireland**. During her term in the [13]**presidency**, Robinson brought more liberal viewpoints to traditionally conservative politics. Apart from efforts in the field of politics, Robinson also [14]**devoted** herself to fighting against poverty and HIV in [15]**Africa**.

Another [16]**remarkable** woman is Angela Merkel. In 2005, Merkel became the first female [17]**Chancellor** of Germany. According to the survey, Merkel was regarded as the most admired German leader since 1949. Merkel, for her iron wills, was also selected to be one of the most powerful women in the world by *Forbes* magazine.

Mary Robinson

Angela Merkel

Cristina Fernandez de Kirchner

In 2007, the former first lady Cristina Fernandez de Kirchner was elected as President in her own right in [18]**Argentina**. Cristina Fernandez, a [19]**senator** and lawyer, making many voters excited about her visions for the country's future, won a [20]**landslide** victory in the election.

All in all, the successes of Merkel, Robinson and Fernandez have proven that women will surely become powerful strengths in world politics.

> *see WORD BANK FOR READINGS*
> *page 156-157*

Reading Comprehension

According to the passage on the left page, choose the most appropriate answers to the following questions.

_____ 1. What is the main idea of the passage?

(A) There have been evil and greedy males blocking women in politics.

(B) There have been politically powerful women in human history.

(C) There have been various voting system in different elections.

(D) There have been famous presidents in every country.

_____ 2. Why does the Viking King suppose his wife should work behind him only?

(A) He thinks he should be the one who makes all the decisions.

(B) He enjoys hiding her from the world.

(C) He finds he feels dizzy when looking out across the sea.

(D) He believes his wife is not doing her duty at home.

_____ 3. What is the difference between Queen Elizabeth I and Joan of Arc?

(A) One was in France; the other was in Germany.

(B) One was a huge success; the other was a big failure.

(C) One was respected by her army; the other was hated by the church.

(D) One was a ruler in her country; the other was an army leader.

_____ 4. What is the common trait among today's three female political leaders?

(A) They are devoting to fighting against HIV in Africa together.

(B) They are ranked as super icons by _Forbes_ magazine.

(C) They are thrilled about the landslide victories in their own countries.

(D) They are embraced in affection of the public and attention of the world.

_____ 5. Which of the following statements is FALSE?

(A) All the women mentioned have shown excellence at their best.

(B) Strength of character is a key factor for these remarkable women to shine.

(C) At present, this world has become female-dominated.

(D) Female leaders can be liberal and active as they intend to.

Providing Examples: Part II
提供例證（二）

1. 使用提供例證的方法時，例子的來源(source)大致可分為：

    a. 經驗或觀察：敘述或描述個人發生的事件或親身的體驗。

    b. 其他消息來源：主要包括科學數據、社會事實，或他人話語等等。

2. 在呈現例證時，可依循以下順序(order)排列：

    a. 依事件發生時間(time)先後：通常最早發生的先敘述。

    b. 依事件發生所在空間(space)位置：可由遠而近，或是由近而遠。

    c. 依事件本身重要程度：可從最重要到最不重要，或從最不重要到最重要。

3. 在提供例證時，可在例子之前適當使用轉接詞(transitional words)，協助讀者了解論點和例子之間的關聯。常用的有：for example, for instance 等。

Drills: In each of the following paragraphs, [1] separately mark out its main idea and supporting examples; [2] outline its source type and presenting order and, if any, highlight the transitional words.

1. It is now common for women to take part in the military forces of some countries. In Taiwan, for example, females were permitted to serve in the army starting in 1991. In 2002, a female military officer was promoted as a general for the first time in this country.

2. While most governments offer new mothers much time, new fathers are not always that lucky. In China, new mothers are given up to 90 days of paid leave, but there is no policy for fathers. In the United States, neither mothers nor fathers get paid time off to spend with their new child.

3. There are numerous problems in the information age. For instance, some people gradually lose direct contacts with their relatives and friends. Others are laid off from their jobs due to computer automation. The worst part lies in that privacy is disturbed or even invaded because personal records can be available in computerized databanks.

WRITING CORNER : GRAMMAR

Avoiding Improper Use of Pronouns: Part II
避免不當使用代名詞（二）

1. 關係代名詞引導形容詞子句，修飾前方所指稱的名詞，具有立即補充說明前方名詞性質的作用。

2. 關係代名詞在形容詞子句中可以作為主格(S)，代稱人使用 who，代稱事物則使用 which。關係代名詞亦可以作為受格(O)，代稱人使用 whom，代稱事物則使用 which。若無特殊情況，以上的關係代名詞都可用 that 取代。

3. 使用關係代名詞時，後方形容詞子句的說明部分要盡量精簡，避免產生句子冗長，造成難以理解的狀況。

4. 如果形容詞子句太長時，就將此子句抽出，另外再起頭寫成一個新的句子。

Drills: In each of the following paragraphs, find out improper use of relative pronouns, and then rewrite the sentences into appropriate forms.

1. Paternal leave, which is given to fathers in Portugal and Spain for only three weeks, to fathers in Guatemala for only two days, and to fathers in China and in the United States for even no one single day, seems to be greatly differently ruled in various countries.

2. Joan of Arc, who was a French teenager, was acknowledged as one of the most inspirational women in history, led the army to confront their British enemy and finally freed her country, and was named a Saint by the church for her contribution to France, has been much portrayed in literary works, in paintings, and even in modern motion pictures.

3. A custom-made yacht, which is decorated with a leather interior and velvet fabrics, built with a swimming pool and a helicopter platform on the bridge, set with the latest nautical locating system and digital stereo equipment, colored with the avant-garde and state-of-the-art paintings, packaged with all the management and technical maintenance, costs a hefty 20 million for a boat of 30 meters, with a million tacked on for every extra meter.

"You can advance work from anywhere!"

❶ SOHO (Small Office, Home Office) 家庭小型辦公室	❹ online booking 網路下訂	❼ handmade accessory 手工製飾品
❷ teleworking/telecommuting *n.* (利用電腦)遠距工作	❺ website *n.* 網站	❽ freelance/freelancer *n.* 自由撰稿者
❸ e-marketing system 電子行銷系統	❻ home-baked cake 家庭烘焙蛋糕	❾ no-frills cosmetics 無多餘裝飾或包裝的化妝品

CONVERSATION I

Chris (C) is coming into the classroom, and his two classmates, Jimmy (J) and Sandra (S), are talking and laughing aloud.

C : *Hey, you guys look sort of excited. What are you chatting about?*

J : *Oh, Chris, we're discussing a good way to make a big fortune on our own.*

C : *A big fortune? You must be kidding. How is it possible to get rich as we're just students?*

S : *Come on, Chris. We're living in the* [1]**digital** *world. Just use your brains, okay?*

C : *So, are you going to take part-time jobs as salespersons in the computer store?*

J : *Of course not, you silly. We're going to build up a website to sell our services.*

C : *Sounds cool. I think a website should be set up only to search for something new and fun.*

S : *Well, actually, we're going to do a real business online for making money.*

J : *That's right. Our plan is to establish a website for editing reports in English. And our target customers will be students who have trouble with their English ability but need to write reports in English.*

S : *Of course, above all, we'll charge a fee each time they use the system for editing their reports.*

C : *Wow, what a fabulous idea! Right now I can think of about at least 20 students needing it.*

J : *No problem. After we build up our system online, just bring them all.*

C : *Wait, since you're going to run a big business, you must need help. Why not count me in?*

S : *That's true. But,* [2]**on second thought**, *we need to find a much smarter partner, if we're going to make a profit.*

C : *Hey, you two have already started talking like* [3]**snobbish** *businesspersons!*

Words and Phrases

1. digital [ˈdɪdʒɪt!] *adj.* 數位的

2. on second thought　重新考慮之後

3. snobbish [ˈsnɑbɪʃ] *adj.* 勢利的

Listening Practice

Listen to the following questions or statements, and choose the most appropriate responses.

_____ 1. (A) Welcome to the talk show tonight.
   (B) About our trip to Paris next week.
   (C) Whom are you talking to?
   (D) Yes, are you available?

_____ 2. (A) The truck blocked our way.
   (B) The Webster's Dictionary is huge.
   (C) Really? Sounds interesting.
   (D) Don't try to build up a castle.

_____ 3. (A) The world has changed, you know.
   (B) About US$100 or a bit more.
   (C) More than enough is too much.
   (D) Why do you have to charge him?

_____ 4. (A) They've got to do something about it.
   (B) English people are troublesome.
   (C) Students are always troublemakers.
   (D) I have no trouble at all.

_____ 5. (A) No, he is not working part-time.
   (B) The party last night went very well.
   (C) The police are always busy.
   (D) Sure. I need to pay for my tuition next term.

CONVERSATION II

🎧 Henry (H) is busy doing his tasks in the study room, and Chris (C) is coming in.

C : *Dad, you know what? I'm going to make money on my own! You and Mom won't call me a* ¹***money-consuming*** *machine again!*

H : *Making money on your own? Wait, son, you mean you won't attend school from now on?*

C : *Not like that, Dad. I just want to be a free and rich SOHO worker like you.*

H : *Well, I see. But, son, what is it that makes you think so?*

C : *Oh, I've heard my classmates discussing a great idea for gaining dollars! But they were unwilling to let me in, saying I wasn't smart enough! I'm thinking about doing it by myself.*

H : *Ha, my son, don't be that naïve. In fact, being a SOHO worker is not as easy and fun as it seems.*

C : *Why is it? You can sleep till noon, and you don't have to be jammed in* ²***hustle-bustle*** *traffic. And, you can have your own schedule. You've got no boss minding your business.*

H : *Yeah, son, that's something* ³***superficially*** *cool. But the truth is: being a SOHO worker is* ⁴***exhausting****! Didn't you ever find me* ⁵***mingling*** *my life and my work all the time?*

C : *Mm.... Now you remind me. I often see you writing piles of drafts in* ⁶***haste*** *until very late. And you've got to consider your work even when you're taking a bath or watching TV!*

H : *That's it. Also, I've got to be totally independent, as I don't have support or resources like people in the company. What's worse, if I find no customers, I could starve to death.*

C : *Wow, Dad, sorry, now I think it is much better to be a student only. After all, it's lucky to get* ⁷***allowances*** *from you and Mom without worrying too much.*

H : *Hey, son, I wonder who says you're not smart enough in making money?*

Words and Phrases

1. money-consuming [ˈmʌnɪ kənˈsumɪŋ] *adj.* 會花錢的
2. hustle-bustle [ˈhʌs!ˈbʌs!] *adj.* 忙碌喧鬧的
3. superficially [ˌsupəˈfɪʃəlɪ] *adv.* 表面地
4. exhausting [ɪgˈzɔstɪŋ] *adj.* 耗費精力的
5. mingle [ˈmɪŋg!] *v.* 使相混
6. haste [hest] *n.* 匆忙
7. allowance [əˈlaʊəns] *n.* 零用錢

Oral Practice

Part I: Blank-filling dialogues

❶ A: Evan, how I want to be a free and rich model like you.

B: Oh, Emma, what is it that makes you ▚▚▚▚▚▚▚▚▚▚▚▚?

A: Well, I've heard you ▚▚▚▚▚▚▚▚ the good chances of ▚▚▚▚▚▚▚▚▚▚▚! But the model agent is ▚▚▚▚▚▚▚▚ to let me in, saying I wasn't tall ▚▚▚▚▚!

B: Ha, my dear, don't be that ▚▚▚▚▚▚▚. ▚▚▚▚▚▚▚, being a model is not as easy and fun ▚▚▚▚▚▚▚▚▚▚▚.

❷ A: The ▚▚▚▚▚▚▚ is: being a freelance photographer is ▚▚▚▚▚▚▚▚! Didn't you ever find me ▚▚▚▚▚▚▚ my work and my leisure all the time?

B: Now you ▚▚▚▚▚▚ me. I often see you taking piles of pictures until very late. And you've got to ▚▚▚▚▚▚ your work even when you're singing in the KTV!

A: That's it. Also, I've got to be ▚▚▚▚▚▚▚▚▚▚. What's worse, if I've got no ▚▚▚▚▚▚, I could ▚▚▚▚▚▚▚▚▚▚.

Part II: Open discussions

❶ Do you want to be a SOHO? Why, or why not?

❷ How do you feel about students starting a business on their own?

SOHO Success

Do you want to be your own boss? Do you hate leaving home for work? Do you enjoy eating and working at the same time? Do you constantly worry about your family while you're working? Do you have brilliant ideas but have no [1]**handsome** money to realize them?

If you answered "yes" to any of these questions, then you are a perfect [2]**candidate** for [3]**initiating** your own SOHO business.

In the first place, you need to have a small office or a home office. Actually, you can even forget to think about getting any small office outside, because having a home office is not only saving your money but also making you just "feel at home." The bathroom, the lawn, or even your [4]**skateboard** will become an ideal working place for your own sake.

After getting a good place to work, you need a great idea most. The great idea will set you apart from other similar SOHO workers in the market. To appeal to more customers than ever, the idea should be as novel as toys made of toilet paper, or as [5]**exotic** as [6]**underpants** made of plastic materials. Always keep in mind that only a great idea can bring in a huge amount of profits.

Of course, [7]**nowadays**, you need a super powerful computer if you desire to succeed as a SOHO worker. The computer will help take orders and make replies to your clients

immediately. In addition, a well-built website will help promote your ideas and display your products to millions of [8]**Internet surfers** as your [9]**potential** buyers around the [10]**globe**.

Anyway, follow these simple steps, and you can turn yourself into a quick and smart SOHO businessperson. And who knows, maybe you will be the next SOHO [11]**billionaire**, while you are taking a nap in bed, or reading a storybook to your son on a beautiful afternoon.

> *see WORD BANK FOR READINGS page 157*

Reading Comprehension

According to the passage on the left page, choose the most appropriate answers to the following questions.

_____ 1. What is the main issue discussed in the passage?
  (A) An interesting program for audience.
  (B) An alternative mode for working.
  (C) An entertaining display of skateboards.
  (D) An unexpected effect on the Internet.

_____ 2. In the first paragraph, what can be inferred from a series of questions?
  (A) A lot of workers in modern days enjoy hating their bosses.
  (B) We can be working better with our better half every moment.
  (C) Family will surely be a terrible obstacle for work.
  (D) People should consider their personalities when choosing a carcer.

_____ 3. Which is NOT one of the steps the author offers to be a SOHO worker?
  (A) Selling only underpants and toilet.
  (B) Looking for a home office or a small office.
  (C) Coming up with a brilliant idea.
  (D) Buying a computer with great functions.

_____ 4. What may a SOHO worker probably look like?
  (A) He or she may get buried in the pile of documents in the office.
  (B) He or she may drink a pint of beer with people shouting around.
  (C) He or she may have a net meeting in bed.
  (D) He or she may shed tears in front of the tomb.

_____ 5. Which of the following statements is TRUE?
  (A) A small office outside is surely less expensive than a home office.
  (B) It costs nothing to become a SOHO worker in today's world.
  (C) Customers are likely to be attracted to smart and bright ideas.
  (D) Internet users can never be a real buyer in the real world.

EXTENDED READING I

[1]Tuna, [2]Moon Cakes, and a SOHO Dream

According to a survey from the Taiwan government, 27% of women in the country lack professional skills to start a business, 22% are short of money, 17% gain no [3]access to market information, and 12% have no [4]confidence in [5]career planning.

However, the [6]statistics have no obvious effects on Hsu, Hsin-chun and Cheng, Ju-yi, two mothers who met at the parent-teacher [7]conference. Before long, the two ladies had come up with the idea of selling the expensive [8]otoro variety of tuna online from their hometown, a fishing village of Tungkang in Taiwan.

In the first month, their business brought in NT$500,000, and in the second month, income totaled NT$800,000. Until the fishing season ended in June, they saw no reason for their business to dry up. Therefore, the two ladies created [9]frozen otoro dumplings that could be sold all year round.

Later on, neither of them got really satisfied—Ms. Hsu and Ms. Cheng used otoro to make moon cakes for the Moon Festival. These treats contained less fat and sugar than traditional moon cakes, and customers were crazy about their interesting products. Before knowing it, these two smart mothers had orders for 50,000 moon cakes!

The case of Ms. Hsu and Ms. Cheng is just one of the growing number of women who work at home or online while taking care of their family in the [10]meantime. In Taiwan, women with similar ideas are [11]inclined to be successful, partly because of the government-aiding programs, like the Small Office Home Office (SOHO) Association and the Flying Geese Program.

The organizations not only provide start-up money to women, but also offer [12]training in marketing, employment, and e-trade. Best yet, they supply social networks for these women to share their thoughts, emotions, and even responsibilities.

The successful 50,000-mooncakes-selling story has [13]inspired many women in need of a fair job and enough time for their family. SOHO working is one of the best [14]options they can take into consideration.

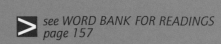

> *see WORD BANK FOR READINGS page 157*

Reading Comprehension

According to the passage on the left page, choose the most appropriate answers to the following questions.

_____ 1. What is the theme of the passage?

(A) A store located on the website.

(B) A product that fails to sell well.

(C) A story of success in SOHO working type.

(D) A program causing serious consequences.

_____ 2. In the first paragraph, what does the author imply with the statistics?

(A) Women now have the best chance to start their own business.

(B) Females are able to own a career even if they have no skills.

(C) The government shows great concerns about family life of women.

(D) There are some problems against females on their working conditions.

_____ 3. Which is NOT one of the means the two ladies took to make a fortune?

(A) Providing living otoro to the aquarium.

(B) Selling expensive otoro variety of tuna online.

(C) Using otoro to make moon cakes for the Moon Festival.

(D) Offering frozen otoro dumplings.

_____ 4. What may be found in government-supported plans for SOHO workers?

(A) Information on money-losing methods.

(B) Instructions on effective promotion for products.

(C) Knowledge of wonderful landscapes.

(D) Guidelines on useful laundry tips.

_____ 5. Which of the following statements is TRUE?

(A) Most females that start a business do not need any financial aids.

(B) The author takes a positive attitude to SOHO working.

(C) The example of the tuna moon cakes actually cannot last long.

(D) The Flying Geese Program is not operated by the government.

Thanks to the rapid growth of digital technology, the number of SOHO workers has kept growing for the last two decades. The word SOHO stands for "small office, home office," and as the name [1]**implies**, anyone can work only at home or just at a small office rather than in a large company.

SOHO Working, So Easy?

With a computer, a fax machine, or even a telephone, anyone can become a SOHO worker, taking a different job from [2]**conventional** work in the office, such as a freelancer, a [3]**broker**, a website designer, or a personal shopper.

However, a SOHO worker must be diligent and independent, as there is no boss around to supervise. Many SOHO workers find it [4]**challenging** to ignore the [5]**distractions** lying around. For example, TV is the most difficult to miss, and the desire to [6]**sneak** off to the kitchen for a snack is always there.

On top of that, a SOHO worker has got to work harder than anyone else in a regular office, for he or she lacks support and resources the company may provide. Therefore, SOHO workers must have confidence in their services, ideas, or products for making a profit. Also, it is [7]**vital** for a SOHO worker to efficiently meet [8]**deadlines** on projects, or customers will be [9]**unpleased**.

With open schedules and [10]**irregular** incomes, a SOHO worker is always faced with the pressure of surviving in the SOHO business. As a result, a SOHO worker must well organize working files and money matters so that his or her business can remain [11]**profitable** for a long time.

Anyway, free and flexible as it may seem, earning one's living as a SOHO worker actually cannot be as easy as imagined.

see WORD BANK FOR READINGS page 157

Reading Comprehension

According to the passage on the left page, choose the most appropriate answers to the following questions.

_____ 1. What is the main idea of the passage?
  (A) There are quite a few risks to be a SOHO worker.
  (B) There are numerous customers around the globe.
  (C) There are the latest hi-tech devices in progress.
  (D) There are enough resources that companies give.

_____ 2. Which is NOT one of the necessary qualities to be SOHO workers?
  (A) They must be independent and diligent.
  (B) They must work harder than those in company offices.
  (C) They must well organize files and money for a long business.
  (D) They must meet the demands from their bosses and neighbors.

_____ 3. Which can be the most challenging against the SOHO working style?
  (A) There used to be confident customers.
  (B) There ought to be too much desire to eat snacks in the kitchen.
  (C) There may be irregular or unstable income sources.
  (D) There should be conventional work in the office.

_____ 4. What may probably be a typical look of a SOHO worker?
  (A) A teacher holding the microphone speaks loudly in the classroom.
  (B) A designer wearing a dress draws in the conference room.
  (C) A broker talking on the earphone wears shorts at home.
  (D) A manager reading the chart gives an order in the office.

_____ 5. Which of the following statements is FALSE?
  (A) A SOHO worker still needs to work efficiently to meet deadlines.
  (B) One of the greatest advantages of SOHO working is tight scheduling.
  (C) The growth of technology enhances convenience for SOHO working.
  (D) SOHO workers can be faced with unimaginable pressure.

Describing a Process: Part I
描述過程（一）

1. 使用描述過程的方式發展段落，是為了解說某件事的進行步驟(steps)或是運作程序(procedure)。

2. 描述某個事件的進行過程可分為以下兩個階段：

   a. 首先，應該在文章中説明要討論的主題。有時甚至必須針對描述對象提出適當而明確的定義(definition)。

   b. 接著，應該依照平常習慣的完成順序(order)依項説明實行該事時應該採取的步驟或流程。

Drills: In each of the following paragraphs, separately mark out its topic and order for explaining a process.

1. If you want to be a successful SOHO worker, the following are necessary measures to take. First, you need to find a small office or a home office. Then, you have to come up with great ideas for gaining the most profits. Next, you need to get a super, powerful computer as a good helper.

2. The two SOHO mothers developed their business step by step. They first tried to sell the expensive otoro type of tuna online. After that, they created novel frozen otoro food, like dumplings and moon cakes. Finally, the two ladies opened a substantial store to sell their otoro food series.

3. The following is an efficient method for memorizing a new word. If you use a dictionary for the new word, remember to get its definition first. Then you should speak out the word several times and pay attention to its pronunciation. Finally, make an example sentence with the word quickly.

4. Do you want your puppies to sleep well at night? Try these tips. First, put a ticking clock beside your little pets, making them feel like still part of their mothers. Next, place a thick, warm blanket nearby, letting them feel safe and sound. Last, be sure to turn off light, and leave them alone.

Avoiding Incorrect Use of Countable or Uncountable Nouns: Part I
避免不正確使用可數或不可數名詞（一）

1. 英語中指稱人事物的字詞稱為名詞(noun)。

2. 所有名詞均可分為「可數名詞」(countable noun)，或是「不可數名詞」(uncountable nouns)。

3. 可數名詞的基本定義為「可以計數的名詞」。因此使用可數名詞時，務必清楚寫出表示該名詞數目只有一個的單數形(singular form)，或是數目超過一個的複數形(plural form)。

4. 不可數名詞的基本定義為「不可以計數的名詞」。因此使用不可數名詞時，不用再考慮單數形或複數形。

5. 寫作時若對某一個名詞是可數或不可數有疑惑，應該勤查字典，不宜隨意猜測或僅憑常理判斷。

Drills: In each of the following paragraphs, find out incorrect uses of countable and uncountable nouns, and correct them into right forms.

1. With computer, fax machine, or even telephone, anyone can be SOHO worker, taking different job from general office works, such as freelancer, broker, website designer, or personal shopper. Apparent feature is that SOHO worker is independent, as there is not even boss to supervise.

2. After getting good place to work, you need great idea. To appeal to as many customer as possible, the idea should be as novel as toy made of toilet papers, or as exotic as underpant made of plastic material. Always remember only great idea can bring in great amount of profit.

3. According to the figure released by the governments, animal were used in 3.1 millions medical experiment in Japan last year, increase of 2.3 percent from the single previous years. Most animal included in experimental procedure were mouse, rat, and livestocks. The increases was mainly because the numbers of genetically modified animal were included.

"We can only be famous for 15 minutes."

❶	paparazzi	*n.* 狗仔隊
❷	celebrity	*n.* 名人，名流
❸	publicity	*n.* 知名度
❹	fame	*n.* 名氣；名聲
❺	camera	*n.* 相機
❻	snapshot	*n.* 快照，快拍
❼	stalk	*v.* 跟蹤
❽	chase	*v.* 追逐
❾	tabloid	*n.* 八卦小報
❿	gossip	*n.* 八卦
⓫	sensational	*adj.* 聳動的

CONVERSATION I

🎧 **26** **Laura (L) and Henry (H) are walking hand in hand out of her office. A news reporter, Vivian (V), and a photographer, Greg (G), are approaching.**

V : *Excuse me. Are you Mr. and Mrs. Parker?*

L : *Ur.... Yes. Mm.... Do we know you, miss?*

V : *Hello, Mr. and Mrs. Parker. I'm Vivian Su. I'm a reporter for Banana Daily News. I've been waiting for several hours. May I ask you some questions? It won't take you too long.*

H : *You've been waiting for hours? Well, maybe we can....*

L : *Wait, Henry. I'm afraid we can't, Ms. Su. We must leave immediately for something important. And, I don't accept sudden* **¹inquiry** *from someone I don't know. You may book an appointment with my personal assistant, and we'll see what we can do.*

V : *Since so, let me put it straight. Mrs. Parker, we've heard that you've been VERY close to your sales manager, Benjamin Li. Have you two got an* **²intimate** *affair?*

H : *What? An intimate affair with Benjamin?* **³Nonsense!** *My wife and I....*

L : *Honey, no need to answer anything. Look, Ms. Su, this is too rude and* **⁴ridiculous**.

V : *Mrs. Parker, I'm JUST doing my job. How actually will you respond to this question?*

L : *I refuse to make comments on any* **⁵insulting** *questions.... Wait, what are you doing?*

G : *Don't* **⁶overreact**. *I'm just taking a few photos of you two.*

H : *Okay, you've* **⁷overstepped** *the borders. You news people had better stop what you're doing.*

G : *We can't help it. We're JUST doing our job.*

L : *Fine! Let's* **⁸put it into law**. *You just wait for a* **⁹lawsuit** *notice from my lawyer.*

Words and Phrases

1. inquiry [ɪnˋkwaɪrɪ] *n.* 詢問
2. intimate [ˋɪntəmɪt] *adj.* 有親密關係的
3. nonsense [ˋnɑnsɛns] *n.* 胡說，胡扯
4. ridiculous [rɪˋdɪkjələs] *adj.* 荒謬的
5. insulting [ɪnˋsʌltɪŋ] *adj.* 侮辱的

6. overreact [ˌovɚrɪˋækt] *v.* 反應過度
7. overstep [ˌovɚˋstɛp] *v.* 踰越；超越限度
8. put it into law   訴諸法律
9. lawsuit [ˋlɔˏsut] *n.* 訴訟

Listening Practice

(27) **Listen to the following questions or statements, and choose the most appropriate responses.**

_____ 1. (A) I'm afraid you are mistaken.
         (B) Sorry, I'm not that handsome.
         (C) Why do you lie to me?
         (D) Never make any excuses.

_____ 2. (A) Leaves are falling in this season.
         (B) I need a medium size.
         (C) It's okay. May we talk later?
         (D) Don't believe words in the media.

_____ 3. (A) Nope, today is July 25th.
         (B) Sure, no problem, go ahead.
         (C) Can I use a question mark here?
         (D) Do you want to have some more fish?

_____ 4. (A) There's always chain reaction in science.
         (B) He is head over heels right now.
         (C) I never overslept before.
         (D) Because I'm upset by the shock.

_____ 5. (A) I've been waiting for the mail deliverer passing by.
         (B) Don't call her waitress but server.
         (C) The car is not ours.
         (D) Don't waste food or money.

CONVERSATION II

🎧(28) **Chris (C) is chatting with his classmate, Thomas (T), in the classroom, and his other classmate, Dolly (D), is walking fast to come around.**

D : *Hey, you boys. Anyone see my Banana Daily News today? I need it right now!*

T : *What do you need the newspaper for? You need to clip some articles?*

C : *Dolly, I wonder why you always eagerly hunt for the newspaper as soon as you come to class?*

D : *You have no idea how important Banana Daily News is. It's my* ¹**food for thoughts**!

T : *Food for thoughts? Are you out of your mind? The tabloid newspaper is totally full of sensational and untrue stories! It should be your food for dark thinking, right?*

C : *Yeah, I agree. The newspaper has indeed caused stress and* ²**chaos** *in society.*

D : *Oh, my, you people really have no sense of humor. In today's world, what else can be more interesting than digging out secrets and* ³**scandals**? *See, here's a good example over a family of a* ⁴**bossy** *CEO mother, a useless coward father, and a stupid son* ⁵**fooling around**.

T : *Wait, here's also a photo of them. The boy looks quite familiar.... He seems to be....*

C : ⁶**Gosh**, *it's me! I can't believe they've* ⁷**covered up** *a photo of my family! How could it be?*

D : *Ha, so, Chris, does your mom really have something to do with her male* ⁸**colleague**? *Does your dad really get* ⁹**pocket money** *from your mom? Are you actually a rich* ¹⁰**womanizer**?

C : *Oh, Dolly, stop it! Don't tell me you believe in those* ¹¹**absurd** *false reports!*

D : *Come on, it does no harm to tell us more about your family, does it?*

T : *Hey, gossip girl, if you keep on being* ¹²**snoopy** *like those tabloids, soon everybody will hate you as "Paparazzi Queen!"*

Words and Phrases

1. food for thoughts　精神食糧
2. chaos [`keɑs] *n.* 混亂
3. scandal [`skændl] *n.* 醜聞
4. bossy [`bɔsɪ] *adj.* 跋扈的，好指使人的
5. fool around　遊手好閒，無所事事
6. gosh [gɑʃ] *interj.* 啊，糟了
7. cover up　報導
8. colleague [`kɑlig] *n.* 同事
9. pocket money　零用錢
10. womanizer [`wumən,aɪzɚ] *n.* 玩弄女性的男子
11. absurd [əb`sɝd] *adj.* 荒謬好笑的
12. snoopy [`snupɪ] *adj.* 好探人隱私的

Oral Practice

Part I: Blank-filling dialogues

❶ A: I ▓▓▓▓▓▓▓▓▓▓▓▓▓▓ you always ▓▓▓▓▓▓ watch *Purple Spider's Web* ▓▓▓▓▓▓▓▓▓▓ you get home?

B: You ▓▓▓▓▓▓▓▓▓▓ important the program is. It's my ▓▓▓▓▓▓▓▓ ▓▓▓▓▓!

A: Are you ▓▓▓▓▓▓▓▓▓▓? The lousy program is totally full of ▓▓▓▓▓▓ ▓▓▓▓▓▓ stories! It should be your food for ▓▓▓▓▓▓▓▓▓▓, right?

B: Oh, my, you really have no ▓▓▓▓▓▓▓▓▓▓. What else can be more ▓▓▓▓▓▓▓▓ than ▓▓▓▓▓▓▓▓▓▓▓▓▓▓?

❷ A: Adie, does Iris really ▓▓▓▓▓▓▓▓▓▓▓▓▓▓ a married guy? Does Ann really get pocket money from you? Is your sister ▓▓▓▓▓▓▓▓ a rich man-eater?

B: Oh, Bruce, stop it! Don't tell me you ▓▓▓▓▓▓▓▓▓▓ those ▓▓▓▓▓▓▓▓ ▓▓▓▓▓▓ rumors.

A: Come on, it does ▓▓▓▓▓▓▓▓▓▓ to tell me more about your life, does it?

Part II: Open discussions

❶ How do you feel about the tabloid media and their reports and photos?

❷ What will you do if a tabloid reporter says he or she wants to interview you and take pictures of you on the street?

⑳ The Paparazzi[1] Profiles

It is no longer safe to go out at night.

Walking down the street, you get a strange feeling that somebody is following you. As you slowly slide your key into the door, you are blinded by flashlights behind the bushes. Your worst [2]**nightmare** comes true!

No, it is not an armed robber. It is a crazy reporter that has just snapped your picture. The paparazzi have struck you again!

The name "paparazzi" is the plural of the Italian word "paparazzo," which means an [3]**annoying** insect. It is a suitable description for these [4]**photo-takers** who never stop following famous people, seizing their private pictures, again and again.

The paparazzi are paid handsome money by the tabloid media to photograph celebrities at their worst. Whenever celebrities are shopping at the mall, relaxing at the beach, or even just standing near the open window, they can never get rid of the paparazzi.

One reporter was paid US$150,000 to snap an intimate moment between Jennifer Lopez and Ben Affleck at her home. In another famous [5]**incident**, Britney Spears attacked some of the paparazzi with an umbrella, after they kept tracking her down, then taking a picture of her new haircut. In other cases, the paparazzi have even took to the skies in [6]**helicopters** to lock onto their targets.

Sometimes, the paparazzi go too far indeed, and they have always been [7]**sued** around the world for creating false stories and for [8]**invading** [9]**privacy**. The death of Princess Diana in 1997 was mostly blamed on those crazy [10]**pursuits** from the paparazzi. On that night, in an attempt to escape from the [11]**crazed** reporters, Princess Diana's car crashed in the tunnel of [12]**Paris**.

However, the news photos from the paparazzi are not always bad. In fact, the paparazzi keep celebrities famous in the news media, so they are often-welcomed guests at major [13]**opening nights** for movies and concerts. Without the paparazzi, these events would not have the right "[14]**buzz**."

Whether you love the paparazzi or hate them, the paparazzi are always there to catch your action, even when you least expect it.

▷ see WORD BANK FOR READINGS
page 157-158

Reading Comprehension

According to the passage on the left page, choose the most appropriate answers to the following questions.

_____ 1. What is the main idea of the passage?
   (A) Narration of the paparazzi over fame and wealth.
   (B) Explanation of the tabloid media on the death of the paparazzi.
   (C) Introduction to the paparazzi and their job.
   (D) Definition of the word "paparazzi" in the dictionary.

_____ 2. Why does the author think "paparazzi" suitable to describe the job?
   (A) The paparazzi take a flight above like annoying insects.
   (B) The paparazzi keep bothering celebrities like annoying insects.
   (C) The paparazzi raise a lot of annoying insects.
   (D) The paparazzi look small and awful like annoying insects.

_____ 3. Why do celebrities probably still love the paparazzi?
   (A) They keep throwing stones at these famous people.
   (B) They blind these famous people with flashlight.
   (C) They seize private pictures of these celebrities.
   (D) They make these celebrities more famous in the news media.

_____ 4. Which is NOT what the paparazzi do?
   (A) They express their pity to the celebrities they have reported.
   (B) They crazily pursue a moving target for snapping a photo.
   (C) They get amazingly high pay from the tabloid media.
   (D) They buzz around major opening nights for movies and concerts.

_____ 5. Which of the following statements is FALSE?
   (A) The paparazzi take pictures of celebrities for their worst images.
   (B) Princess Diana's death was greatly blamed on the paparazzi.
   (C) Ben Affleck and Jennifer Lopez were snapped in their private time.
   (D) Britney Spears was nice to the paparazzi for praising her new haircut.

WHO'S BEHIND THE PAPARAZZI?

"Madonna was [1]**witnessed** beating out her husband on the street!"

If you read a newspaper headline like this, would you believe it? Perhaps you would not, but as a matter of fact, thousands of people read, and even believe, such a kind of news report.

The tabloid press, well known for its [2]**catchy**, [3]**stirring** headlines to attract its readers, hires the paparazzi photographers to take pictures of celebrities secretly in their [4]**embarrassing** situations. On top of that, the tabloid press is filled with juicy gossip and shocking rumors, though mostly on the basis of false facts, yet [5]**selling like hot cakes** for multi-million dollars.

A good example is *The Sun*, the best-selling daily newspaper in [6]**Britain**. The tabloid paper has kept spying into details and seeking for scandals of celebrities' private affairs. However, its readers seem to always come back for more. Actually, America's [7]***The National Enquirer*** and Taiwan's *Apple Daily*, using similar tricks in news [8]**presentation**, have also been successful in their sales.

Nevertheless, the tabloid press has been under serious [9]**criticism**. Most celebrities claim the tabloid reports do great harm to their careers, and even to their lives. In 1997, a photographer was said to [10]**tailgate** Princess Diana's car so crazily that she was killed in the [11]**tragedy** of a car accident in Paris. British people turned this sorrow and anger against the paparazzi and the tabloid press.

Even if you do not believe the [12]**tall tales** in the tabloid press, do you think they are harmlessly fun? Do you think celebrities are fair subjects for hunting by the paparazzi? Should these famous people [13]**deserve** all the chasing stuff and the [14]**distorted** reports? Or else, do you think the paparazzi, along with the tabloid press behind, have created

killing dangers and have torn people's lives apart?

Either way, whenever you find a tabloid paper lying around, you will probably pick it up, and have a quick look through, no matter what you think of the paparazzi and the tabloid press cultures behind it.

> *see WORD BANK FOR READINGS*
> *page 158*

Reading Comprehension

According to the passage on the left page, choose the most appropriate answers to the following questions.

_____ 1. What is the main idea of the passage?

(A) Readers of tabloid papers should believe the reports and pictures.

(B) The tabloid press is mostly responsible for the paparazzi culture.

(C) The paparazzi can seize more photos to spice up the stories.

(D) Celebrities deserve to be badly treated because they are rich.

_____ 2. Which is NOT one of the means that the tabloid press takes in their reports?

(A) Baking hot cakes.   (B) Talking juicy gossips.

(C) Making catchy headlines.   (D) Spreading shocking rumors.

_____ 3. Why arc the tabloid newspapers successful in their sales?

(A) The tragedy of Princess Diana in Paris destroyed the tabloid culture.

(B) The vendor machines on the streets have been disappearing.

(C) Their readers long for more sensational details and scandals.

(D) Their print factories shut down more often on holidays.

_____ 4. What causes the paparazzi to be criticized?

(A) They are beneficial to the bright career of celebrities.

(B) They make distorted stories and tear people's lives apart.

(C) They use expensive cameras and drive high-class cars.

(D) They are sad and angry after every car accident.

_____ 5. Which of the following statements is TRUE?

(A) The paparazzi are fair subjects for hunting by the celebrities.

(B) It is the paparazzi that deserve all the spying and chasing stuff.

(C) However people feel about the tabloid papers, they just go for them.

(D) The tabloid press has got to lower down the prices for selling.

EXTENDED READING II

Confession from the Paparazzi

Sometimes I hate my job.

Last week, I was waiting outside Paris Hilton's house. I was sitting across the street, camping on top of the small hill with a perfect view of her front door. My last meal was over ten hours ago at breakfast. I was tired, hungry, and oh, my, it started raining....

Around 2 a.m., I was about to pack up my camera when I saw a light coming on inside the house. Through the window, I could see a woman walking into the room, only wearing a towel. Wait...it's her!

Suddenly, she dropped her towel to the floor, [1] **totally** naked!

SNAP! I just took a photo that would pay for my next six months.

At that time, I loved my job.

I'm a paparazzi photographer. I take photos of celebrities at the moments they least want me there. Then, I sell the pictures to the tabloid press. The more revealing the photos, the more money! If there's good drama on the spot, like a pop star fighting with his girlfriend, that'll be even better!

Although the celebrities I follow may live an exciting life, mine is [2] **desperately** boring. I spend most of my days following tips to find a celebrity. I drive all around town, I get lost, and when I finally arrive, I have to find a good place to hide. Once I've located the star, I've got to wait. And wait.

Some nights all the celebrities come out to attend movie [3] **premiers** or award shows. On these nights I know where to find the stars, but I have to fight against all the other paparazzi to get the best shot. I've got to take hundreds of photos before I pick up the one that will sell.

Living dangerously can also be a job [4] **hazard**. More than one star has come running after me in a [5] **rage** after I've snapped a photo. Sometimes their dogs or [6] **bodyguards** do that too.

However, I've never thought about quitting. I keep coming back for more because the [7] **thrill** of capturing those sensational images is hard to be replaced.

> *see WORD BANK FOR READINGS*
> *page 158*

Reading Comprehension

According to the passage on the left page, choose the most appropriate answers to the following questions.

_____ 1. What is the theme of the passage?

(A) Training to be the pro paparazzi.

(B) Pricing on photos taken by the paparazzi.

(C) Illustration on the life patterns of the paparazzi.

(D) Solution to the problems of the paparazzi.

_____ 2. Which may be one of the advantages of being a paparazzi photographer?

(A) He or she may get hungry all day long to pass out.

(B) He or she may enjoy being chased by dogs and bodyguards.

(C) He or she may fight with a celebrity's boyfriend.

(D) He or she may make a big fortune for taking fabulous pictures.

_____ 3. Which is NOT one of the working challenges that the paparazzi face?

(A) They can get as many signatures from celebrities as they want.

(B) They often need to wait long hours for a good snapshot.

(C) They will probably live an extremely plain and dull life.

(D) They must fight with other paparazzi to seize the best shot.

_____ 4. Why does the narrator want to keep working as a paparazzi photographer?

(A) He or she has been used to attending movie premiers.

(B) He or she cannot resist the excitement of shooting thrilling pictures.

(C) He or she enjoys hiding in a good position out of the public.

(D) He or she only has the skill to earn a living.

_____ 5. Which of the following statements is FALSE?

(A) The paparazzi have got to be equipped with a camera.

(B) The paparazzi must practice keeping track of their targets.

(C) The paparazzi are definitely welcomed by all the celebrities.

(D) The paparazzi live most of their lives tensely for shooting pictures.

Describing a Process: Part II
描述過程（二）

1. 使用描述過程方法發展段落時，應該依循以下的原則：

    a. 可使用表達指示語氣的祈使句(imperative sentence)解說步驟。

    b. 正確並且簡要地描述實行步驟內容。

    c. 採用分解步驟的方式，說明完成過程的程序。

2. 在描述過程時，應該適當使用轉接詞(transitional words)串連整個過程的各項步驟。最常使用的包括：first, then, next, after that, last 等。

Drills: In each of the following paragraphs, [1] separately mark out its topic and the order for explaining a process; [2] outline every step of the process in discussion and, if any, highlight the transitional words.

1. Here is how the paparazzi generally work for a snapshot. First, they spend a whole day tailgating celebrities. Then, they wait for a chance to take sensational photos of the famous. Next, after they get something good, they soon sell the photos to tabloids at a fair price.

2. Some celebrities revealed how to cope with the paparazzi well. First, they take it easy to respond to any action the paparazzi take, showing they do not care at all. Next, they give out some messages for the paparazzi to have for a bite. Then, they just walk away, smiling goodbye.

3. If you see someone suffering from electric shock as he or she grabs a live wire, remember not to touch the person. Instead, first, watch out if you are standing on the wet ground. Next, take a totally dry cloth to carefully snatch the wire and cast it aside from the person. Then, check if the person is still breathing. If not, exert CPR on the victim right away. Meanwhile, call the ambulance as soon as possible.

Avoiding Incorrect Use of Countable or Uncountable Nouns: Part II
避免不正確使用可數或不可數名詞（二）

1. 如果使用可數名詞作為主詞，務必注意單數名詞需對應使用表示單數的動詞型態。同樣的，複數名詞作主詞時，需對應使用表示複數的動詞型態。

2. 如果使用不可數名詞作主詞，則動詞部分需使用單數型態。

3. 值得注意的是，使用動詞時，除了考慮主詞本身是否為可數名詞之單數或複數，或是不可數名詞之外，還需要配合正確的時態，才能造出適當完整的句子。

Drills: In each of the following paragraphs, find out incorrect uses of countable or uncountable nouns and their corresponding verbs; then correct them into right forms.

1. The most notorious example was *The Sun*, which are Britain's best-selling daily newspaper. Reader seem to love seeing it gossiping and spying into private detail of celebrity, so they always comes back for more. Indeed, America's *The National Enquirer* and Taiwan's *Apple Daily* has been successful in sale figure since similar trick get taken in their news.

2. The paparazzi is paid a lot of moneys to photograph celebrity when they shows their worst. Reporter is paid US$150,000 several year ago as he snap private moment between Jennifer Lopez and Ben Affleck. Whether celebrity are shopping at the mall or relaxing at the beach, they were never safe from the paparazzi.

3. U.S. team of several biologist have found out the truths that mankinds often detect sexual attraction by sniffing at certain amount of physical chemical of other. The physical chemical mainly come from pheromone, widely known as the sex hormone which are released by possible mate. As signal is sent to identifying center in the brain, the brain perceive it as specific odor or smell.

"Mr. Rogan, let's do Unit Five today."

❶ teacher-centered *adj.* 以老師為中心的	❺ obedient *adj.* 服從的	❾ active *adj.* 主動的
❷ lecture *n.* 講課	❻ student-centered *adj.* 以學生為中心的	❿ participating *adj.* 參與的
❸ authority *n.* 權威	❼ group work 分組活動	
❹ passive *adj.* 被動的	❽ advisor *n.* 顧問	

CONVERSATION I

Chris (C) is sitting on the fence outside the classroom, and his classmate, Fiona (F), is talking with him.

C : *Just my luck! I can't see why Mr. Tsai kept* ¹***picking on*** *me today!*

F : *Oh, Chris, stop* ²***whining*** *and don't take it personal. We know Mr. Tsai well. Usually he's nice. Perhaps he was a little bit too serious about what you did in class.*

C : *A little bit too serious? I think he was "OVER" serious! I just pointed out there might be an error in his word choice. Then he got mad, saying I was* ³***finding fault with*** *him!*

F : ⁴***No hard feelings****. That's because a teacher in Taiwan is thought to be a source of knowledge and authority. So it's generally considered disrespectful to voice a doubt about the viewpoints of your teacher.*

C : *But in the States, many teachers, especially in college, are close to students, sometimes even like our friends! We're always encouraged to ask questions or give opinions anytime in class!*

F : *I know that. But teachers here are expected to show a strict image. So, if you* ⁵***stand in Mr. Tsai's shoes****, perhaps he was quite* ⁶***stressed out*** *when you suddenly did that without discussing your question with him* ⁷***beforehand****.*

C : *Mm.... I never thought of that. Now I think your words somehow make sense.*

F : *Since so, Chris, why not go have a private talk with Mr. Tsai? This is a good chance for you to know more about teachers in Taiwan.*

C : *Well, I'm afraid Mr. Tsai is still unhappy. Maybe he doesn't want to talk to me.*

F : *I don't think so. Mr. Tsai is a good teacher, and you two deserve to know each other more, right?*

Words and Phrases

1. pick on　挑剔；找麻煩
2. whine [hwaɪn] v. 發牢騷
3. find fault with　挑…的缺點；指責
4. No hard feelings.　別生氣了。
5. stand in one's shoes　站在某人的立場；替某人設身處地想
6. stressed out　承受壓力的
7. beforehand [bɪˋfor͵hænd] adv. 事先，提前

Listening Practice

Listen to the following questions or statements, and choose the most appropriate responses.

_____ 1. (A) Don't grab me while I'm walking.
(B) Good idea. I'm hungry too.
(C) My mother is glad to buy that for you.
(D) Don't bite off more than you can chew.

_____ 2. (A) He belongs to the basketball team.
(B) I never thought about I could find this again.
(C) You can be a good leader.
(D) She's doing her job. Don't take it personal.

_____ 3. (A) He's not my child.
(B) He can speak several languages.
(C) His parents teach him well.
(D) He's really a good instructor.

_____ 4. (A) Yeah, and she's quite nice and serious.
(B) Don't forget to hand in your report tomorrow.
(C) Teaching is an excellent job.
(D) I'm glad you like teaching.

_____ 5. (A) It depends on how much it is.
(B) I live on the next street.
(C) Thank you for praising my dress.
(D) The deadline of my book is getting closer.

CONVERSATION II

🎧 **Chris (C) is meeting his ¹instructor, Mr. Tsai (T), in Tsai's office.**

C : Good morning, Mr. Tsai. Thank you for giving me a chance to talk with you.

T : You're welcome. In fact, I also would like to discuss last week with you.

*C : To be honest, Mr. Tsai, I felt bad after your class for a while. And I almost decided not to attend your class anymore. Yet, Fiona advised I had better discuss the whole thing face to face with you to ²**clear up** possible misunderstandings.*

*T : Well, that's good. Numerous huge conflicts in human history ³**stem from** a little ⁴**spark** of misunderstanding. Actually, I lost my temper a bit that day, and I am sorry.*

C : Please don't say so. But would you please tell me why you got that angry with me?

T : Well, the course schedule is tight and we need to finish so much in only one semester. I have to keep our class at a fast pace. So, it's simply not a right time in class to tell me anything about word usage, and you corrected me in a loud tone. I felt stressed out at that time.

C : Now I see. But sometimes I really can't stand the way class is conducted here. There's almost no interaction between teachers and we students.

*T : I know that. However, in Taiwan, teachers are always required to be responsible for ⁵**academic** performance of students. Most teachers are ⁶**toiling** on for their teaching missions, just like me.*

C : I understand better now. Thank you for sharing all these with me.

T : I'm happy to talk with you more, too. Well, by the way, remember to hand in the final report on schedule, and please tell the others to do so for sure.

C : Yes, Sir!

Words and Phrases

1. instructor [ɪnˋstrʌktɚ] *n.* 大學講師
2. clear up   澄清
3. stem from   源於
4. spark [spɑrk] *n.* 一點點，絲毫
5. academic [͵ækəˋdɛmɪk] *adj.* 學術的
6. toil [tɔɪl] *v.* 辛苦工作

Oral Practice

Part I: Blank-filling dialogues

❶A: Good morning, Ms. Lin. _____ to be in your talk show.

B: You're welcome. _____, I would like to discuss the speech you gave in the stadium yesterday with you.

A: _____, Ms. Lin, I felt bad after the speech _____. And I almost _____ your show for now. Yet, my working staff _____ I _____ the whole thing _____ _____ with you to _____.

❷A: Would you please tell me why you _____ me?

B: Well, the cargo _____ and we need to finish so much in only one week. I have to keep our production _____. So, it's simply _____ by now to tell me anything about your yearly leave, and you notify me _____. I _____ at that time.

Part II: Open discussions

❶ If you were misunderstood by your teacher, or you had a disagreement with your instructor, how would you handle the conflicts? Why?

❷ From your poin t of view, what should the best teacher-and-student relation be like? Why?

Passing the Test, but Failing the Conversation ?

Teacher A says, "Take out your notebook and a pen. I'm going to give a lecture on **structural** design." In another classroom, teacher B says, "Ok, class, each group has 40 short sticks and 40 centimeters of tape. You'll have 30 minutes to build a structure. Then I'll see whose structure can hold up the most weight."

In which class will you choose to be?

Teacher A's classroom is typically teacher-centered. The advantages of this learning style include quick **instillation** of information, a quiet and **orderly** classroom, and easy testing. However, students are likely to memorize facts than to understand ideas. That is the reason why many English learners receive high scores on tests, but fail to keep a simple conversation going on.

On the other hand, teacher B is leading a student-centered classroom. In this learning type, students are trained to develop personal abilities, and are required to apply the skills they have learned to real-life situations. Such was the case for 15-year-old Hina Saifi of **India** when she found herself giving a speech in English without notes to over 150 people, just two years after she started learning this way.

However, as students are taught to figure out simple principles a teacher offers, the student-centered learning takes much longer time. Besides, classrooms of this type are often loud and **disorderly**, because students are busy with team projects or group activities. Also, testing is difficult because students **construct** a knowledge base in their own way instead of learning a list of facts and figures.

Which approach is better?

When answering the question, consider the following situation: You must climb to the top of a ten-meter structure. One was built by someone who has read a lot about design, but has no hands-on experience for building. The other one was built by somebody who has never read books on design, but has a lot of experiences in building.

Which structure would you rather climb?

see WORD BANK FOR READINGS
page 158

Reading Comprehension

According to the passage on the left page, choose the most appropriate answers to the following questions.

_____ 1. What is the theme of the passage?
   (A) Two different building structures.
   (B) Two different learning methods.
   (C) Two different speaking principles.
   (D) Two different testing skills.

_____ 2. Which is one of the advantages of the teacher-centered learning?
   (A) An ability of one's own.   (B) A team in the project.
   (C) A skill applied to real life.   (D) A test easily given.

_____ 3. Why is testing difficult in the student-centered learning?
   (A) Students take part in too many team activities and projects.
   (B) Teachers require the classroom to include a strong structure.
   (C) Students build up the base of knowledge in their own way.
   (D) Teachers have hands-on experience in memorizing facts.

_____ 4. What can be inferred from the two different types of classrooms?
   (A) Students behave themselves in the student-centered classroom.
   (B) There are fewer interactions in the teacher-centered classroom.
   (C) Students in the student-centered classroom usually score high.
   (D) Activity design is a required course in the two types of classrooms.

_____ 5. Which of the following statements is FALSE?
   (A) Hina Saifi could speak Engllish fluently in front of many people.
   (B) Quick instillation of information helps memorize facts.
   (C) The student-centered classroom is noisy because of group projects.
   (D) There are more lectures in the student-centered classroom.

(38) Same Love, 900 Years Afar

A female teacher, Mary Kay Letourneau, made the most [2] **shocking** headline of 1997 in the United States, for she had an affair with her 13-year-old boy student, and she even got pregnant with him. Letourneau was then put in prison. In 2004, Letourneau was released, and finally she married her student in 2005.

As a matter of fact, it was not a brand-new love story between a teacher and his or her student. A similar story took place more than 900 years ago in France, starring one of the best known couples in history, Abelard and Eloise.

Peter Abelard was a famous and handsome [3] **philosopher** in Paris. Abelard fell in love with the 13-year-old beautiful girl, Eloise, 20 years younger than he. To get close to Eloise, Abelard told her uncle he wanted to be her tutor. With all the difficulties, it was not long before Abelard made Eloise his lover.

When Eloise became pregnant, the affair could no longer be hidden. The two lovers ran away, and later, they secretly got married. However, Eloise's uncle was so angry that he had Abelard [4] **castrated**.

In the end, Abelard became a monk, while Eloise became a nun. The lovers saw each other only once after that, but their love was kept alive in their romantic letters for 20 years. In one of the letters, Eloise said she felt no regret for the love with Abelard: "Only love given freely, rather than the bond of a marriage tie, is significant to an ideal relationship."

Six hundred years later, Josephine Bonaparte ordered the remains of Abelard and Eloise to be buried together at the [5] **Cemetery** of Père-Lachaise. Until today, lovers keep visiting the [6] **tomb** and leaving flowers in honor of their great romance.

Looking back from now, perhaps too few of us can really stop to think why the female teacher, like a modern Abelard, far from being admired for her strong passion, would find herself in jail over her true love with her boy student.

> see WORD BANK FOR READINGS
> page 158

Reading Comprehension

According to the passage on the left page, choose the most appropriate answers to the following questions.

_____ 1. What is the topic of the passage?

(A) Important conferences between teachers and students.

(B) Daily conflicts between females and males.

(C) Intimate relationships between teachers and students.

(D) Culture shocks between females and males.

_____ 2. Why are the two couples known to the world?

(A) Both of them wrote wonderful love letters.

(B) Both of them have children of their own.

(C) Both of them met in the Europe.

(D) Both of them fell in love in an unconventional way.

_____ 3. What were the endings of the two couples in love?

(A) One got hurt; the other died.

(B) One got lost; the other arrived.

(C) One got disappointed; the other smiled.

(D) One got together; the other departed.

_____ 4. In the last paragraph, what does the author imply?

(A) The story of Latourneau and her student should be printed out.

(B) The example of Abelard and Eloise should be checked out.

(C) The case of Latourneau and her student should be understood.

(D) The pain of Abelard and Eloise should be eased.

_____ 5. Which of the following statements is TRUE?

(A) Eloise and Latourneau were put in jail for a period of time.

(B) Abelard and Eloise are remembered for their romance until today.

(C) Abelard and Bonaparte were severely punished for their deeds.

(D) Latourneau and Bonaparte were buried at the cemetery in the States.

Learning More Than from Books

Chang Yuan-chih, an 18-year-old student of the [1]**Holistic** Education School, set a record as the youngest mountain climber in Taiwan who *successfully climbed up the [2]**Aconcagua**, the highest mountain (6962m) in Argentina of South America. Chang completed the difficult task after he took a required mountain climbing course in school.

What school would rule mountain climbing as a required course? What training did Chang receive that enabled him to carry a 30-kg [3]**backpack**, walking in a snowstorm with 20 degrees [4]**Celsius** below zero?

The answers come from non-traditional, [5]**innovative** [6]**alternative** [7]**schooling**.

Chang had been learning to be independent in school all the time, and he managed to raise funds and organize the difficult journey by himself. Both self-discipline and [8]**creativity** are the keys to Chang's success.

The major difference between traditional schools and alternative ones lies in the way students are treated and educated. In some alternative schools, students are usually given broad instructions for a project and are left to figure out details on their own. In others, students are also partly responsible for setting rules and for planning courses.

Generally speaking, students in alternative schools have much more freedom as individuals. For example, a student in Forest [9]**Elementary** School of Taiwan may walk away from the group to sit alone under a tree during outdoor science class if he or she wants to.

Summerhill School in Britain may be the [10]**forerunner** of alternative schools. Founded in Germany in 1921, Summerhill was moved to England two years later. A. S. Neill, the [11]**founder** of the school, was [12]**convinced** that children could do their best when they were not forced to learn. In that school, [13]**attendance** was [14]**voluntary**, and students were welcomed to help govern the school by voting on new rules and policies.

Although successful cases keep coming up, there are some students from alternative schools failing to fit into the conventional test-focusing education. However, because of the creative skills they have learned before, most students can [15]**adjust** to the new situations, and [16]**eventually** can do very well. It is proven again that innovative learning methods can produce positive learning results.

---

*Based on Chang's opinion, the phrase "successfully climbed" is preferred to the word "[17]**conquered**." For Chang, conquering is not the real value to finish climbing the mountains. Chang said he took the challenge just because he wanted to learn to [18]**coexist** with Mother Nature.

see WORD BANK FOR READINGS page 158

Reading Comprehension

According to the passage on the left page, choose the most appropriate answers to the following questions.

_____ 1. What is the main purpose of the passage?

(A) To welcome the votes on new rules and policies.

(B) To give broad instructions to teachers and students in school.

(C) To convince children to climb high mountains.

(D) To explain the benefits of innovative alternative schooling.

_____ 2. What did Chang Yuan-Chih do for climbing the Aconcagua?

(A) He walked away from the group and sat alone.

(B) He raised funds and organized the journey.

(C) He served as a voluntary worker and did well.

(D) He took an exam and planned a course.

_____ 3. Why did A. S. Neill found Summerhill School?

(A) To adjust to the new environment.

(B) To have less individual freedom.

(C) To let children not forced to learn.

(D) To fit into test-focusing education.

_____ 4. What can be inferred concerning students in alternative schools?

(A) They all take a required mountain climbing course.

(B) They usually develop more creativity.

(C) They are fully responsible for school policies.

(D) They always fail in tests and exams.

_____ 5. Which of the following statements is FALSE?

(A) Students are left to find answers on their own in alternative schools.

(B) Summerhill School was founded in Germany in 1921.

(C) Most students in alternative schools can fit into conventional schools.

(D) Positive results can only be produced by traditional learning.

Comparing & Contrasting: Part I
比較和對比（一）

1. 使用比較和對比的手法發展段落，可以顯示兩個相關主體(subjects)之間的相同點(similarities)或相異點(differences)。

2. 一般說來，「比較」和「對比」的基本定義是：「比較」指的是「呈現相同點」，而「對比」指的是「呈現相異點」。

3. 使用比較和對比的方式時，往往必須同時討論主體的相同點和相異點。

Drills: In each of the following paragraphs, separately mark out its main idea and points of comparing or contrasting.

1. There are two types of classroom. One is teacher-oriented, whose advantages contain quick instillation of information and a quiet and orderly classroom. The other is student-oriented, whose strong points include strong motivation for learning and interesting interactions.

2. The difference between traditional schools and alternative ones is in their educational ways. In traditional schools, students have few instructions and should obey the orders from teachers. Yet, in alternative schools, students are offered broad instructions to figure out details on their own.

3. Some people work as they need to make a living. People of this kind usually dislike their jobs, keeping complaining till the end of the day. Nevertheless, some other people enjoy doing their jobs. These people typically show great passions for work, and stick to it to the last minute.

4. At one glance, there is something in common between bats and birds. Both of the two flying animals have wings on their sides. However, they are greatly different in the way they give birth to the offspring. Birds lay eggs and hatch them into infants, while bats take a similar path to the other mammals.

WRITING CORNER : GRAMMAR

Avoiding Improper Use of Passive Voice: Part I
避免不恰當使用被動語態（一）

1.「被動語態」是相對於「主動語態」的語意表達方式。「主動語態」的句子主詞是「動作的產生者」，而「被動語態」的句子主詞是「動作的接受者」。

2. 使用英語時，應優先考慮主動語態。若是沒有特殊或是必要的狀況，就不應該隨意使用被動語態，否則容易造成動作產生者置於句尾而不明顯。

3. 句子使用被動語態的主要時機如下：

　a. 句子未能出現動作產生者時。

　b. 句子意圖強調動作接受者時。

Drills: In each of the following paragraphs, identify whether passive voice is properly used or not. If not, rewrite the improper parts into appropriate forms.

1. Headlines were made by a teacher, because a love affair had been had by her with a 15-year-old boy student. Society was indeed shocked by the case. Yet, it is not viewed as a brand-new story, as a similar event was found more than 900 years ago in France. The real, sad love story was starred by a world's famous couple, Abelard and Eloise.

2. Teacher A's classroom is called teacher-centered. Lessons of much information, a quiet and orderly classroom, and easy testing are included as the advantages of the teaching style. However, facts are often memorized by students, but ideas are seldom understood by them. Then, high grades in English are received by many English learners, while a simple conversation cannot be kept going by them.

3. It is reported that iPods were chosen by students over clubs as their favorites. The fancy, high-tech digital kit was placed much higher than social gathering by students from 145 colleges. Because of the boom of the Internet, clubbing has been kicked out of the list of the five most frequent recreations. Popularity is garnered by iPods this time mainly because lectures can be downloaded to be reviewed anytime.

"We are all made of flesh and blood. It shouldn't matter what sex you choose to love"

1. **LGBT pride parade**
女同性戀(Lesbian)、男同性戀(Gay)、雙性戀者(Bisexuality)、跨性別者(Transgender) 遊行

2. **gay** *n.* 男同性戀者

3. **lesbian** *n.* 女同性戀者

4. **bisexuality** *n.* 雙性戀者

5. **transgender** *n.* 跨性別者

6. **LGBT-friendly** *adj.*
對 LGBT 友善的

7. **anti-LGBT** *adj.* 反對 LGBT 的

8. **homophobic** *adj.* 恐懼同志的

9. **come out (of the closet)**
出櫃 (同性戀者公開表示自己的性向)

10. **mask** *n.* 面具

11. **drag queen**
扮裝皇后 (男扮女裝的反串秀主角)

12. **rainbow flag** 彩虹旗

13. **float** *n.* 遊行用花車

CONVERSATION I

Henry (H) and Laura (L) are coming home together, and they see Chris (C) sitting on the sofa.

H : *Hey, son, we're home. How's your day? Is everything in school okay?*

C : *Dad, leave me alone! I don't want to talk about it!*

L : *Calm down, Chris. You sound mad and look awful. What's wrong with you, son?*

C : *Let me tell you what happened. One of my best friends, Joseph, said he liked me VERY much.*

H : *What's wrong with that? Your best friends should like you, or else?*

C : *It's not like that, Dad. Joseph meant he wanted to be my...mm...lover!*

L : *I see. But, son, what's the big deal with Joseph's love* [1]***confession***?

C : *Mom, you have no idea how scared I got! It felt like the whole world stopped* [2]***spinning***! *I could even hear my own* [3]***heartbeats***! *I couldn't breathe, and I...I....*

H : *Chris, I think you REALLY need to calm down for a while.*

L : *Son, I think I have to ask you what happened next?*

C : *Ur.... Ur.... I yelled, "Get away from me!" And I ran away as fast as I could.*

H : *Then, you must have hurt Joseph's feelings. He's your best friend, isn't he?*

L : *I think your Dad is right. Would you be frightened if it were not Joseph, but a female best friend making a confession to you?*

C : *Mm.... I know what you mean, Mom. To be frank, I feel upset about what I've done to Joseph. He's been nice to me, and we have a good time together.*

H : *Since so, why not try to have a* [4]***man-to-man*** *talk with Joseph to tell him how you feel?*

C : *I know. A* [5]***heart-to-heart*** *talk seems much better. I hope it won't be too late.*

Words and Phrases

1. confession [kən`fɛʃən] *n.* 自白；坦白
2. spin [spɪn] *v.* 旋轉
3. heartbeat [`hɑrt,bit] *n.* 心跳
4. man-to-man [`mæntə`mæn] *adj.* 坦率的
5. heart-to-heart [`hɑrttə`hɑrt] *adj.* 開誠布公的

Listening Practice

Listen to the following questions or statements, and choose the most appropriate responses.

_____ 1. (A) I feel sorry to hear you say so.
(B) I can deal with the problem.
(C) The information is new to me.
(D) It's a report on a terrible earthquake.

_____ 2. (A) You need to buy a new towel.
(B) You need to calm down for a while.
(C) Let the child be quiet.
(D) Don't stand there too long.

_____ 3. (A) You turned the wrong direction.
(B) Your daughter will go later.
(C) My car broke down on the road.
(D) Here comes his dog.

_____ 4. (A) Maybe she should study further.
(B) Perhaps she enjoys performing.
(C) Maybe she was in a bad mood.
(D) Perhaps she forgot sending the package.

_____ 5. (A) Well, I should donate some for charity.
(B) I don't like wooden furniture.
(C) The butter tasted so rich.
(D) The medicine is out of reach.

CONVERSATION II

Joseph (J) is playing basketball alone, and Chris (C) is coming up slowly.

C : Ur.... Hi, Joseph, are you okay, ur...no, ur.... How are you?

J : Hi, Chris, how are you? What's up? You don't sound like the usual you.

C : Joseph, would you mind having a talk with me for a while?

J : Absolutely not. Go ahead. I'm curious about what makes you this ¹**anxious**.

C : Ur.... I want to apologize for what I did when you made your...mm...love confession to me.

J : Well, it's no big deal. In fact, you're not the worst one to do something like that.

C : What? You mean you ever ²**confessed** to other...ur...men? And they did something worse?

J : Yeah, I'm human, so I need to look for a mate too. I had a good boyfriend for almost a year. One day, he shouted, "I don't want to be gay!" From then on, he just disappeared.

C : I'm sorry to hear that. You must have been hurt. How could he do that?

J : You haven't seen anything yet. I remember when I expressed love to a good friend in high school, he kicked me down on the ground, roaring at me, "You ³**pervert**! Get out of my sight!"

C : Mm.... I can imagine you must have tasted bitter tears all alone.

J : Well, actually, yes. But after so many years, my tears have ⁴**drained out**. It's tiring to be gay in this world, so I don't want to get hurt again from anybody's twisted thinking.

C : Well, like me. I'm sorry. You know, I don't think I can afford to lose a good friend like you.

J : Well, stop saying sorry, okay? I'm glad to see you start thinking of me as a real friend. So, dare to play basketball with me?

C : Ha, of course. You'd better watch out. Here I am!

Words and Phrases

1. anxious [ˈæŋkʃəs] *adj.* 焦慮的
2. confess [kənˈfɛs] *v.* 自白；坦白
3. pervert [ˈpɝvɝt] *n.* 性變態者；行為反常者
4. drain out　流乾

Oral Practice

Part I: Blank-filling dialogues

❶ A: I want to ░░░░░░░░░░░░░░░░ what I did when you ░░░░░░░░░░░░░░░░ ░░░░░░░░░░ to me.

B: Well, it's ░░░░░░░░░░░░░░. ░░░░░░░░░, you're not the ░░░░░░░░░░ one to do something like that.

A: What? You mean you ever ░░░░░░░░░░░░ other girls? And they treated you even ░░░░░░░░░?

B: Yeah, I confessed to a good female friend of mine almost a year ago. After I finished talking, she ░░░░░░░░, "I don't want to be with you! And I don't want to see you again!" ░░░░░░░░░░░░, she just ░░░░░░░░░░.

❷ A: I remember when I ░░░░░░░░ my love to a good friend in high school, she ░░░░░░░░░░ me, "Shut up! Get ░░░░░░░░░░░░░░!"

B: I can ░░░░░░░░ you must have ░░░░░░░░░░░░░░░░ for quite a long time.

A: Well, ░░░░░░░░░, yes. But after a few days, I just felt my ░░░░░░░░ had ░░░░░░░░░░░░░░. It's ░░░░░░░░░ to have a crush on somebody, and I don't want to ░░░░░░░░ again from anybody's rejection.

Part II: Open discussions

❶ What will you do if a friend of the same sex says to you, "I want to be your lover?"

❷ How do you think of love relationship between the same sex?

Gay at Great Risk

In 1998, Matthew Shepard was [1]**harshly** beaten and cruelly tied to the fence in a remote area of the western United States. The 22-year-old man remained [2]**dangled** for 18 hours before he was found by a passing bicyclist. It was too late for the bitterly [3]**tortured** young man, who died in mad and [4]**inhuman** violence.

Soon after, a gang of men who [5]**brutally** killed Shepard were caught by the police. When asked why they took Shepard's life, they replied in cold blood, "He's a gay!" The killers are still serving their time in jail for the crime.

In 2007, Human Rights Watch, an international [6]**monitoring** [7]**agency**, [8]**declared** that thousands of people around the globe had been reported to be put to death for being gays since 1979.

The worst example can be found in [9]**Iran**, where any cruel action against [10]**homosexuals** is completely legal. If anyone gets caught in homosexual acts, the punishments will include 175 [11]**lashes** with a whip, plus [12]**severe** torture and long-term [13]**imprisonment**. In 2005, two teenage boys were even publicly hanged just because they [14]**allegedly** had been witnessed in a sexual act.

In contrast, [15]**Canada** may be the nicest country in the world to people whose sexual [16]**preference** is the same sex. Unlike "Don't Ask, Don't Tell" policy on gays in the U.S. military, in Canada, gays and lesbians are allowed to openly serve in the armed [17]**forces**. There are laws against gay [18]**discrimination**, and domestic benefits for same-sex love couples for their [19]**partnership**. In 2005, Canada became one of the few nations that had recognized gay marriages.

However, barriers remain solid elsewhere in the world, [20]**particularly** in [21]**Islamic** countries. In 2006, when [22]**the United Nations** (UN) wanted to [23]**consult** with organizations that work to protect rights of gays and lesbians, the move was badly blocked by Iran, even with the unexpected support from the United States.

Obviously, a world without [24]**homophobia** is still far away for gays.

> *see WORD BANK FOR READINGS*
> *page 159*

Reading Comprehension

According to the passage on the left page, choose the most appropriate answers to the following questions.

_____ 1. What is the theme of the passage?

    (A) Discussion about openness to gay marriage in the United Nations.

    (B) Beneficial policies of the Canadian government for gays and lesbians.

    (C) Service of gays in the army of the Islamic countries.

    (D) Gays and lesbians still face living threats in many parts of the world.

_____ 2. If you're a gay or a lesbian, what kind of rights can you have in Canada?

    (A) Rights to marriage.   (B) Rights to discrimination.

    (C) Rights to violence.   (D) Rights to homophobia.

_____ 3. Which is NOT mentioned as a bad situation against gays and lesbians?

    (A) They were put to death for loving the same sex.

    (B) They may be severely tortured and irrationally imprisoned.

    (C) They are allowed to openly serve in the armed forces.

    (D) They cannot be legal partners in marriages in many countries.

_____ 4. What kind of inhuman deeds against gay men ever occurred in Iran?

    (A) Matthew Shepard was beaten and tied to the fence for hours.

    (B) Two boys were put to death for their possible same-sex behavior.

    (C) Organizations that work for rights of gays were consulted.

    (D) Human Rights Watch warned the government not to bully gay men.

_____ 5. Which of the following statements is FALSE?

    (A) Different countries hold different attitudes to gay issues.

    (B) The United States is reserved in its attitudes to homosexuals.

    (C) The United Nations forcefully protects homosexuals worldwide.

    (D) Canada stands opposite to Iran over policies on homosexuals.

EXTENDED READING I

Gay Pride, from New York to Taipei

On a cold, chilly day in October, men wearing swimming trunks parade through the center of Taipei City, smiling, cheering and waving rainbow-colored flags and ¹**banners**.

This is the typical scene in Taipei's gay pride parades, which started in 2003 and have been ²**annually** held since then. The first event was small, with only 1,000 participants, mostly local gay men. However, the event has been greatly ³**expanding** each year. In 2007, there were around 15,000 participants in the parade and many of them came from abroad to support the ⁴**campaign** together.

The original gay pride movement started in 1969 in the United States. One night, the police arrived at a gay bar in New York called the Stonewall Inn and began to arrest people. Gay bars were illegal then, so gay people were used to such a bad treatment. Usually, they accepted being ⁵**mistreated**, as they felt they had no choice.

However, something changed this time. People in the bar became ⁶**irritated** at the police and their violent means. No one was sure what ⁷**triggered** the action and gay people decided to fight back. Soon after, big fights broke out between gay men and the police. The bar was surrounded by many angry members of the gay ⁸**community**, and the police were forced to hide inside. The struggles went on for several days.

In the following year, a parade was held to remember the events of the year before. This was the first gay pride parade. The struggles around the Stonewall Inn inspired many gays to stop accepting any bad treatment from the government, and to be brave to stand up and fight for their rights instead.

Later on, the ⁹**mode** of the gay pride movement spread out across America and internationally. Gay marches began to be annually held in big cities across the world. Today, there are varieties of colorful gay pride events in many countries where gay rights are valued and respected.

see WORD BANK FOR READINGS
page 159

Reading Comprehension

According to the passage on the left page, choose the most appropriate answers to the following questions.

_____ 1. What is the main idea of the passage?
  (A) Taipei's gay pride parades can not be compared with New York's.
  (B) The Stonewall event was a disaster to the gay community.
  (C) Gay rights can be valued and stressed in parade events.
  (D) Gay groups should not contact the government.

_____ 2. Which is INCORRECT about the gay pride parades in Taipei?
  (A) There are gay men showing up in swimming suits.
  (B) The number of the participants has been decreasing yearly.
  (C) Some participants came from abroad to join the activity.
  (D) Such typical symbols as rainbow-colored banners have been used.

_____ 3. Why did the gay men in the Stonewall Inn have a fight with the police?
  (A) They were badly treated and unreasonably arrested.
  (B) They were too drunk to identify the police staff.
  (C) They were surrounded by many angry members in the community.
  (D) They were forced to hide for several days.

_____ 4. What was the most important lesson that the Stonewall event gave?
  (A) It turned the Stonewall Inn into a famous sightseeing spot.
  (B) It made the government punish the police.
  (C) It expanded the living surroundings of gay groups.
  (D) It inspired many gay men to stand up and fight against mistreatment.

_____ 5. Which of the following statements is TRUE?
  (A) The Stonewall Inn was the only legal gay bar at that time.
  (B) The first gay parade was held before the Stonewall event.
  (C) A few big cities are highly celebrated for their big gay marches.
  (D) The gay parades have been held every two years since 2003.

🎧 ⁴⁷ A World of Difference

Wade Nichols met his partner, Shen, when they were students in the United States. In 2002, they moved to Taiwan to search for jobs, and got married the same year. Shen even made sure their wedding showed a [1]**Halloween** [2]**theme** in honor of Nichols' favorite holiday.

However, now Nichols moves back to the States to attend graduate school, while Shen still stays in Taiwan for work. Nichols and Shen, like many other cross-nation same-sex couples, are facing direct challenges.

Legal conditions make same-sex marriages between people from different countries complicated. In this case, neither Taiwan nor the States officially recognizes their relationship, as same-sex marriages are not [3]**legalized** in these two countries. Even if the couple got married in the Netherlands, where same-sex marriages became legal in 2000, their union will not be recognized either if they travel abroad.

Official [4]**denial** to the relationship has also stripped many gay couples of their legal rights. For instance, a gay man cannot get automatic [5]**insurance coverage** over his [6]**spouse**, and he even cannot get money from the insurance company if his partner dies. In addition, if a gay man needs to have an [7]**operation** in the hospital, his partner will not be allowed to sign up for any vital [8]**documents** as a "legal" mate.

However, there are some places, such as New York City and [9]**Israel**, that do not allow same-sex marriages but have recently decided to recognize those performed somewhere else. As to [10]**Mexico** and Argentina, same-sex marriages are [11]**acknowledged** in some parts of the country, like Mexico City and [12]**Buenos Aires**, but are not recognized anywhere else.

All in all, same-sex couples from different countries still face much more difficulties than [13]**heterosexual** couples. Numerous gay couples have been forced to live thousands of miles apart, because neither of their countries recognizes their marriage. It is obvious that same-sex couples, like Nichols and Shen, will continue fighting for their rights along with their marriages in the future.

➤ *see WORD BANK FOR READINGS page 159*

Reading Comprehension

According to the passage on the left page, choose the most appropriate answers to the following questions.

_____ 1. What is the main purpose of the passage?
  (A) To teach same-sex couples quick access to marriages.
  (B) To describe joys and sorrows of a gay couple in marriage.
  (C) To introduce the wedding ceremony of lesbians.
  (D) To present the difficulties of same-sex marriages in different countries.

_____ 2. Which one is true about lawful acknowledgment of same-sex marriage?
  (A) In Taiwan, only couples of both Taiwanese can be accepted.
  (B) In Mexico, same-sex marriage cannot be registered in law.
  (C) In the Netherlands, same-sex marriage can be legally recognized.
  (D) In Israel, same-sex marriages have been admitted.

_____ 3. Why is marriage substantially significant to same-sex couples?
  (A) They can have a better chance to adopt children.
  (B) They can have the same rights as heterosexual couples.
  (C) They can gain more working opportunities than usual.
  (D) They can travel abroad more rapidly and frequently.

_____ 4. What may NOT be an obstacle that a same-sex couple has to face?
  (A) When one passes away, the other cannot get any compensation from the insurance company as heterosexual mates can.
  (B) When one needs to have an operation in hospital, the other cannot sign up for any important documents for agreement.
  (C) When one wants to find a suitable job, the other plans to go further study in his or her hometown.
  (D) When one attends a gathering for family reunion, the other in company cannot claim to be his or her mate on the occasion.

_____ 5. Which of the following statements is FALSE?
  (A) Marriages are definitely meaningful to same-sex partners.
  (B) Same-sex marriages can't be recognized in laws of New York City.
  (C) The Netherlands has recognized same-sex marriages.
  (D) For gays and lesbians, cross-nation love can be smoother.

Comparing & Contrasting: Part II
比較和對比（二）

1. 使用比較和對比的手法發展段落時，可採取以下的方式呈現討論細節：

   a. 以主體(subject)為重心，同時討論不同特色的相同和相異處。

   b. 以特色(character)為重心，同時討論不同主體的相同和相異處。

2. 使用比較和對比的方法時，可在說明的論點之前適當使用轉接詞(transitional words)，協助讀者了解比較或對比的呈現部分：

   a. 強調「相同點」時，可用 likewise, similarly, in the same way 等。

   b. 強調「相異點」時，可用 however, by contrast, on the contrary 等。

Drills: In each of the following paragraphs, separately mark out its main idea and points of comparing or contrasting and, if any, highlight the transitional words.

1. Taipei's gay pride parades started in 2003 and have been held each year since then on. The first event was small, with only 1,000 participants, mostly local gay men. By contrast, in 2007, it was apparent that the event was largely expanded. There were around 15,000 participants in the parade and many of them came from abroad.

2. Behaviors of same-sex love are differently viewed and treated around the world. Iran may be the worst place, with its legal cruel action to lash, torture, and imprison people caught in homosexual acts. However, Canada could be the best place, with its admission to gay marriages and protective measures to ensure human rights of gays and lesbians.

3. The status of dinner table has greatly changed then and now. In the past, the dinner table was a socially significant place for a family to gather in a fix time at the end of the day, sharing experiences and emotions. On the contrary, nowadays, it is rarely seen a whole family gets together at the dinner table having supper, as modern people are busy all too often.

Avoiding Improper Use of Passive Voice: Part II
避免不當使用被動語態（二）

1. 使用英語寫作時，應優先考量主動語態。如果動作產生者消失，或是必須強調動作接受者時，才應該考慮使用被動語態。

2. 使用被動語態時，須注意下列要點：

   a. be 動詞是否與主詞一致？

   b. be 動詞是否配合文句的時態？

   c. be 動詞後是否使用過去分詞？

   d. 動詞規則和不規則變化的過去分詞拼字是否正確？

Drills: In each of the following paragraphs, find out improper uses of and verbal errors in passive voice, and correct them into right expressions.

1. In 1970, the first gay pride parade were holded to highlight Stonewall Event of 1969. From then on, many gays are persuading that bad treatment from the government should no longer be accepted by them, and that their human rights should be fighted for instead.

2. In 1998, Matthew Shepard is cruelly beated and tieed to a fence in the farm. The poor young man were dangling there for 18 hours before he is finded by a passing bicyclist. In Iran, 2005, two teenage boys were publicly hung, as they are allegeed to have been witnessing in a sex act. Even today, gay men was still hateed and ignoreed in many countries.

3. The Academy Awards was gived out every year to commend outstanding performance of movie workers. These awards was nicknameed Oscars, and was presenting in a formal ceremony in Hollywood. Different people in the film industry was nominateed in certain categories. Though predictions on real winners could be maked before the ceremony, the final results could only be knowed when the envelopes was unsealing.

"Let's Live in LOHAS!"

1. fancy car　華麗大車
2. fur coat　皮草大衣
3. crocodile bag　鱷魚皮包
4. skyscraper *n.* 摩天大樓
5. shark fin　魚翅
6. hybrid small car　汽電共生小車
7. recycled bottle fabric　保特瓶回收布料
8. organic cotton T-shirt　有機棉 T 恤
9. green building　綠色建築
10. organic vegetables　有機蔬菜

CONVERSATION I

Laura (L) and her colleagues, Jasmine (J) and Nancy (N), are having lunch in the restaurant.

N : *Look, girls! A TV news reporter is talking about chaos happening in the shopping mall last night! It was crowded with angry people waiting all night long for a shopping bag!*

J : *Oh, my goodness! These people broke the windows in the stores, pushed down the security guards, and had quarrels and fights with each other!*

N : *That's ¹**incredible**. It's hard to imagine all this happened JUST because of a shopping bag! I start wondering what exactly this ²**troublemaking** shopping bag looks like.*

L : *Well, I've read an article in the fashion magazine about the shopping bag. Actually, that's a plain-looking ³**canvas** handbag, stitched with "I'm NOT A Plastic bag" outside.*

J : *Sounds like a common shopping bag. How come it ⁴**stirred** everybody **up**?*

L : *Mm.... Not exactly. Though it may look usual and normal, it's the latest product sold by a recently noted fashion brand with a ⁵**rising** British designer. And it ONLY costs NT$500!*

N : *Wow, no wonder. But, I can't see why they use "I'm NOT A Plastic bag" there?*

L : *In fact, that's a bit of humor from the designer. The designer said she felt bad seeing ugly and wasteful plastic bags piled in the supermarket. So the smart lady designed this fashionable shopping bag with the ⁶**witty** words to remind people not to use plastic bags anymore.*

J : *Oh, that's it. I'm impressed that fashion design can balance our daily needs with action for the environment.*

N : *It seems we don't need to give up our favorite fashion stuff for environmental purposes.*

L : *Of course we needn't. We modern women love fashion, and we love the planet as well.*

Words and Phrases

1. incredible [ɪnˋkrɛdəbl̩] *adj.* 令人不敢相信的
2. troublemaking [ˋtrʌbl̩ˌmekɪŋ] *adj.* 製造麻煩的
3. canvas [ˋkænvəs] *n.* 帆布
4. stir up　引起(騷動)
5. rising [ˋraɪzɪŋ] *adj.* 行情看漲的
6. witty [ˋwɪtɪ] *adj.* 機智的

Listening Practice

🎧 **Listen to the following questions or statements, and choose the most appropriate responses.**

_____ 1. (A) I bought an apartment recently.
(B) I can not go to the stores with you today.
(C) They're having a big sale today.
(D) There's a windstorm to come.

_____ 2. (A) Right. His Christmas present was impressive.
(B) Me too. He must have made efforts to prepare.
(C) No way. First impression is vital.
(D) Really. There's seldom a presentation about impression.

_____ 3. (A) I know she is witty.
(B) The witch never appears again.
(C) Thank you for finding my coat.
(D) They're nothing new but from Shakespeare.

_____ 4. (A) Oh, I'm sorry I forgot to do that.
(B) Mm, why are you so happy?
(C) Right, I am happy to receive your reminder.
(D) Well, my birthday was two months ago.

_____ 5. (A) A purple car is flashy.
(B) Please fill in the application form.
(C) Mainly on my strong interest in the field.
(D) I went to school yesterday.

CONVERSATION II

🎧 **Laura (L), Henry (H), and Chris (C) are strolling in the shopping mall.**

C : *Mom, this overcoat you bought looks so in and cool.*

H : *Wow, what a day! Our prince is giving praise to the shopping* [1]***captures*** *of our queen.*

L : *I'm really pleased to hear that, son. Why do you think so?*

C : *I remember you wanted to buy some* [2]***environmentally-friendly*** *clothes, but you just worried if they were not fashionable. Now I find out this new overcoat is remade by* [3]***altering*** *and tailoring two different old, already-* [4]***worn*** *coats, but it shows fantastic designs.*

L : *Yeah, isn't it a pleasant surprise? I once thought doing something environmental would be dull and ugly. I probably would have to wear unattractive linen clothes, chewing tasteless* [5]***tofu*** *and organic vegetables all the time! But now environmental issues have been set up into a new trend for designing around the globe. It's become a fashion itself.*

H : *That's true. Like the Taiwanese dishes of organic food we ate the other day, they tasted delicious and looked* [6]***delightful***. *Even the shirt I have on is made from recycled bottles. Can you belive it? Also, don't forget you're wearing a T-shirt of organic cotton without any chemicals used on it. It looks fit and feels comfortable, doesn't it?*

C : *Yeah, I thought I would have nothing to do with any environmental stuff before.*

L : *Not at all now. Trust me. Loving the environment will be an easy lifestyle and a new entertainment in the future.*

C : *Oh, Mom, you're the most* [7]***trend-spotting*** *female I've ever seen.*

H : *Hey, son, you keep* [8]***flattering*** *our queen. Do you want your mom to buy you anything?*

Words and Phrases

1. capture [ˈkæptʃɚ] *n.* 戰利品
2. environmentally-friendly
   [ɪnˌvaɪrənˈmɛntlɪ ˈfrɛndlɪ] *adj.* 減少環境破壞的，對環境友善的
3. alter [ˈɔltɚ] *v.* 修改(衣服)
4. worn [wɔrn] *adj.* 破舊的
5. tofu [ˈtofu] *n.* 豆腐
6. delightful [dɪˈlaɪtfəl] *adj.* 令人愉快的
7. trend-spotting [ˈtrɛndspɑtɪŋ] *adj.* 追蹤流行的
8. flatter [ˈflætɚ] *v.* 恭維

Oral Practice

Part I: Blank-filling dialogues

❶A: I remember you wanted to buy an ████████████████ car, but you just ████████████ if it was not ████████████ . Now I find out your new car ████████████████████████ .

B: Yeah, isn't it a ████████████████? I once thought buying something ████████████ would be ████████████ . I ████████████ would have to drive some shabby-looking stuff on the road ████████████████!

❷A: Now ████████████████ have been set up into a new ████████████ for designing ████████████████ . It's become a ████████████ itself.

B: You bet. Like the Italian ████████████████ we ate the other day, I'm surprised they ████████████████ and ████████████████ . Even the trousers I have on are made from ████████████████ . Can you believe it?

Part II: Open discussions

❶ What have you ever done to help protect the environment?

❷ From now on, what plan do you have to help conserve our planet?

Living in LOHAS

A young, pretty woman is preparing to go for work in the morning. She washes her face with organic cleansers and puts on all-natural make-up. She wears a dress woven from an all-natural [1]**blend**, cleaned with [2]**resolvable** [3]**detergent** in a highly-rated energy-efficient washing machine.

Then, as she locks up the door of the [4]**solar-powered** house, she drives her [5]**hybrid-generated** car to the office, placing a bowl of salad of organic vegetables inside a recycled paper bag down on the passenger's side....

This is my neighbor, Joanna Moore, one of the millions of people who now live in "Lifestyles of Health and [6]**Sustainability**," generally known as LOHAS.

As the name suggests, LOHAS represents environmentally-friendly lifestyles. People who live in LOHAS are devoted to protecting the environment, only buying goods and using products that help keep Mother Earth alive.

With 35 million people in the United States alone and an [7]**estimated** US$208 billion annual [8]**revenue** around the globe, people living in LOHAS have been such a large target market that no company would take a risk to ignore.

Here are some steps to take to join people living in LOHAS.

First of all, when visiting the local supermarket, we can pick organically grown fruits and vegetables without any chemicals used on them. Then, we can choose organic products for our personal care, such as shampoo, facial soap, and lipsticks

made of natural [9]**ingredients** instead of [10]**artificial** [11]**compounds**.

In addition, if we buy a car, a vehicle generated with no gas is [12]**preferable**. Of course, we can [13]**renovate** our house with [14]**renewable** energy sources taken and used, either from the wind, the sun, or from [15]**hydroelectric** power.

Anyway, environmental protection can not only be a social issue, but also be a personal lifestyle. Let's live in LOHAS, and we are sure to see beautiful Mother Earth.

▷ *see WORD BANK FOR READINGS page 159-160*

Reading Comprehension

According to the passage on the left page, choose the most appropriate answers to the following questions.

_____ 1. What is the main purpose of the passage?

    (A) To illustrate a neighbor who lives an alternative life.

    (B) To explain a famous brand that has recently hit the stores.

    (C) To introduce a new lifestyle that is friendly to Mother Earth.

    (D) To discover some rare energy that can be explored today.

_____ 2. Which is NOT one of the living patterns of the author's neighbor?

    (A) Using electric-saving washing machine.

    (B) Walking to the shopping mall in the distance.

    (C) Eating proper amounts of organic vegetables.

    (D) Living in the house powered by solar energy.

_____ 3. Why do people living in LOHAS become a vital target on market?

    (A) Most LOHAS customers only buy goods that are good for earth.

    (B) Many drivers living in LOHAS just use renewable energy for vehicles.

    (C) The natural environment has been changed into lands for building.

    (D) The large LOHAS population brings a remarkable profit.

_____ 4. If someone wants to live in LOHAS, what can he or she do for that?

    (A) He or she can buy organically-made products for personal care.

    (B) He or she can choose vegetables and fruits with chemicals on.

    (C) He or she can drive a car powered by huge amounts of gas.

    (D) He or she can use artificial compounds for everything in life.

_____ 5. Which of the following statements is TRUE?

    (A) The author implies that people living in LOHAS consume more energy.

    (B) The author concludes that LOHAS may have negative effects.

    (C) The author suggests that every house on earth be rebuilt.

    (D) The author implies that LOHAS can be part of daily habits.

🎧(54) Fashion¹ Runway, an²Eco Way

Speaking of the fashion industry, people often hit upon an image that rich customers keep on spending more money than sense, buying ³**glamorous** clothes and ⁴**dazzling** accessories.

Recently, however, many opinion leaders in the fashion business have been taking steps to change the selfish image by promoting environmental concerns with their designs in fashion.

Stella McCartney, daughter of the former Beatles musician Paul McCartney and now even better known as one of the hottest fashion designers, claimed that she, ⁵**absolutely** refusing to use any leathers, would use organic materials in all of her ⁶**creations**.

Actually, Ms. McCartney is not a ⁷**front-runner** in the fashion industry trying to help save the environment. In the 1990s, several famous super models felt pity for animals hunted for their furs, so they gathered to speak against clothes made of fur.

For a while, many people stopped wearing furs. Some brands even stopped selling fur-made products. Even quite a few designers stopped using animal skins in their fashion designs. The campaign seemed to have been successful, though it is a shame that fur clothes have recently become ⁸**trendy** again!

However, it is apparent that fashion designers have become more concerned about the sources of raw materials they use. Some have even been stressing that their products are ⁹**manufactured** on the principle of "fair trade"—workers who manufacture the products, often in poor countries, will be well paid and treated for their ¹⁰**labor**.

¹¹**Ironically**, while so many fashion designers have proudly announced their large use of natural materials, some scientists indicate certain artificial materials may be better for the environment, because innovative fabrics can be effectively washed at lower temperatures, with much less energy ¹²**consumed**.

Anyway, as going "green" is a major trend around the globe, designers and scientists have been trying their best to be a helping strength. Most importantly, it seems that fashion in an eco way will stand a better chance to last this time, instead of being just another passing ¹³**fad**.

▷ *see WORD BANK FOR READINGS page 160*

Reading Comprehension

According to the passage on the left page, choose the most appropriate answers to the following questions.

_____ 1. What is the theme of the passage?
  (A) An innovative fabric that is manufactured into clothes.
  (B) A new trend that balances fashion and environmental protection.
  (C) A brave designer that stops using fur in her creations.
  (D) A rich customer that spends lots of money on fur.

_____ 2. Why do some fashion designers decline using leather and fur for design?
  (A) They want to help save the planet.
  (B) They intend to be more successful in sales.
  (C) They mean to damage their brand images.
  (D) They desire to be fairly treated in the public.

_____ 3. What follows the super model's anti-fur action in the 1990s?
  (A) People wore even more fur-made clothes than ever.
  (B) Some brands started promoting fur-manufactured products.
  (C) Many designers decided not to use fur in their creations.
  (D) Fashion goods in animal skins became much more popular.

_____ 4. What can be concluded from the mention of "fair trade?"
  (A) It is an organization in charge of fashion campaigns.
  (B) It is usually operated in rich countries.
  (C) It is a way to let those who offer the most labor be well-paid.
  (D) It is especially stressed among scientists.

_____ 5. Which of the following statements is FALSE?
  (A) Going "green" means doing everything with ecological concerns.
  (B) Both designers and scientists do their part to keep nature alive.
  (C) Newly developed fabrics can be helpful in saving energy.
  (D) Fashion in an eco way can never be everlasting so far.

🎧 55 THE LIFE CYCLE OF BEEF

To many customers, beef steak is always their favorite when it is an option on the menu. However, has it ever occurred to you that eating beef does more damage to the environment than driving a car?

Indeed, a team of Japanese scientists stated in 2007 that the [1]**production** of a one-kilogram steak creates the same amount of [2]**carbon dioxide** (CO_2) [3]**emission** as a three-hour car drive plus leaving all electric lights on at home!

Taking a closer look at the life cycle of beef, from cattle-raising to steak-eating, you will realize that a huge amount of energy has been lost and wasted.

First, the grain for cattle to eat must be grown and harvested, be treated and packaged, and then be transported to beef farmers. The news on the CNN website reads that one pound of corn makes one pound of bread, two to three pounds create one pound of chicken, four pounds produce one pound of pork, but twelve pounds turn into ONLY one pound of beef!

In addition, [4]**cattle sheds** are lit with electric lights and operated with heavy [5]**machinery**. Later, the meat must be [6]**refrigerated**, packed and transported to the market. Finally, before beef steak is served on the dining table, cooking the beef into delicious steak consumes extra electricity and gas!

In order to reduce the great loss in energy, some groups of farmers believe that returning to the old [7]**farming** ways helps [8]**conserve** energy. In 2003, a [9]**Swedish**-[10]**conducted** study indicated that farming "organic beef" — feeding cows on grass instead of grains—would reduce the regular CO_2 emission by 40% and would consume less energy by 85%.

However, here is another quicker and easier solution that many scientists as well as all [11]**vegetarians** suggest: Eat less beef. By doing so, valuable energy and important resources on the planet can be conserved.

As a result, next time, just think twice before you order a thick slice of steak for a bite, as you have already known the life cycle of beef.

▶ see WORD BANK FOR READINGS page 160

Reading Comprehension

According to the passage on the left page, choose the most appropriate answers to the following questions.

_____ 1. What is the main purpose of the passage?

(A) For urging people to eat less beef to reduce energy loss.

(B) For showing people that cow-raising is a painstaking job.

(C) For informing people of facts and figures on steak houses.

(D) For telling people some good ways to well cook steak.

_____ 2. Which is NOT part of beef production?

(A) Feeding cattle on a good deal of harvested and treated grains.

(B) Running cattle sheds with enough lighting and heavy machinery.

(C) Refrigerating, packing, and then transporting the meat to the market.

(D) Stripping cattle off their skins and washing them clean.

_____ 3. What is farming "organic beef" related to?

(A) It has been reported by a Swiss-sponsored study.

(B) It means feeding cows with grass rather than grains.

(C) It would reduce the CO_2 emission by 90%, with 38% energy saved.

(D) It has been conducted worldwide already.

_____ 4. Why does the author cite the news on the CNN website?

(A) He or she wants to learn to surf on the Internet.

(B) He or she wants to practice counting the amount of corn.

(C) He or she wants to know the recipe for different kinds of meat.

(D) He or she wants to reveal how wasteful it is to eat beef.

_____ 5. Which of the following statements is probably TRUE?

(A) Eating beef would produce less emission of CO_2 than driving a car.

(B) Cooking beef only consumes a little of gas.

(C) One may eat less beef after learning about its production process.

(D) Eating less beef has no influence on energy conservation.

Explaining Causes & Effects: Part I
解釋原因和結果（一）

1. 使用解釋方式(explanatory)發展段落時，需要檢視某個動作或某個事件的原因和結果，以及因果彼此的相互關係(correlations)。

2. 使用解釋原因和結果的方法之前，應該先說明討論的主題，之後再寫出解釋該主題之原因或結果的補充句。

3. 補充句中解釋的原因或是結果都應該以其重要程度(importance)依序呈現。常使用的排列方式是從最重要的論點開始，之後依重要程度遞減呈現；或由較不重要的論點開始，到段落最後呈現一個重要的高潮結束。

Drills: In each of the following paragraphs, separately mark out its main idea and causes or effects for explaining.

1. Much energy has been lost in the grain production for millions of cattle to eat. First, the grain must be grown and harvested. Then it must be packaged and transported to beef farmers.

2. Earlier in the 1990s, fierce action was taken to help save the animal lives. Several famous super models spoke out against fur-made clothes. As a result, people stopped wearing furs, shops stopped selling fur-fabricated products, and designers stopped using animal skins in their fashion lines.

3. Seeking a job is never an easy job. Many job hunters with a good chance in the beginning often cannot gain a new job finally. The main reason lies in that there are some small but vital errors in the interview. First, they may be late for the meeting. Then, they may be improperly dressed. Above all, they may be not fully prepared for all the questions.

4. Watching TV has become a common and easy habit in every household. Nevertheless, programs on TV are now harshly criticized. Lack of originality can be the most serious problem. Non-stop commercials pop up all the time. Next, there come lousy, indecent program productions without careful planning beforehand.

WRITING CORNER : GRAMMAR

Common Use of Acronyms
常用的首字母縮略字

1. 在寫作過程中，為了精簡版面同時吸引讀者注意，往往將原本由數個連續字形成的普通名詞中，每個字開頭的第一個字母抽取出來，另外組合成一個新的英文單字，稱為「首字母縮略字」(acronym)。
2. 頭字語本身可作為名詞使用，亦可作為放在名詞之前的形容詞。
3. 許多頭字語已經成為普遍使用的常見字彙，故寫作時不需要再拼寫全名。
4. 頭字語發音依照使用習慣，分為依序唸出每個字母，或合為一個單字發音。

Drills: The following are several acronyms frequently used in different fields. Figure out their full spellings and identify their meanings.

Field	Acronym	Full Spelling	Meaning
Society	(1) DJ		
	(2) VIP		
	(3) ASAP		
	(4) SOHO		
	(5) LOHAS		
Business	(1) PR		
	(2) CEO		
	(3) GNP		
	(4) WTO		
	(5) APEC		
Science & Technology	(1) PDA		
	(2) LCD		
	(2) UFO		
	(4) CPR		
	(5) HIV/AIDS		
Politics	(1) PC		
	(2) UN		
	(3) EU		
	(4) US		
	(5) WHO		

"Without heart, there can be no understanding among us all."

fireman 消防員

chairman 主席

occupation 職業類別

firefighter 消防員

chairperson 主席

chink 中國奴

negro 黑鬼

Chinese 中國人

race 種族

black/African American 非裔美國人

the crippled 殘障者

the blind 盲人

physical feature 生理特徵

the physically challenged
身心障礙者

the visually challenged
視覺障礙者

dragon lady
難搞定的女人

sissy guy
娘娘腔的傢伙

personal style 個人風格

feminine man
帶有女性氣質的男人

competent woman　　有能力的女性

CONVERSATION I

Chris (C) is playing video games on the stairs in front of the library, and his classmate, Sean (S) is reading a novel beside him.

S : *Hey, Chris. I've heard that you're from the States.*

C : *Yeah, since I was born, my parents and I have lived in* ¹***Chicago*** *until last year. What's up?*

S : *No, just curious. You must have seen a lot of Negroes around there. People say they look as black as coals or chocolate. Is that real? Do they smell* ²***stinky***?

C : *Oh, Sean, you scare me! It's impolite, or I should say it's rude, to talk about black people like that. If you talked that way in the States, you might be making people feel* ³***insulted***.

S : *How come? I looked up the word in the dictionary, and it reads "negro" is referred to "a black person." And it's widely rumored that Negroes...ur...black people are* ⁴***smelly***!

C : *You seem to be* ⁵***misled*** *by* ⁶***ambiguous*** *explanations in the dictionary. In fact, "Negro" is an old-fashioned,* ⁷***offensive*** *word used to refer to a black person. Actually, they preferred to be called "black," and they are now officially named "African-Americans."*

S : *I have no clue on what you're talking about! This is all new to me!*

C : *And, it's not proper to say something about physical or mental traits of people in* ⁸***judgmental*** *expressions, just like "stinky" or "smelly."*

S : *Now I don't know how to talk about some people in English correctly.*

C : *Hey, not that bad. Why not start by changing your old dictionary into an* ⁹***updated*** *one to avoid using offensive terms again?*

Words and Phrases

1. Chicago [ʃəˋkɑgo] *n.* 芝加哥 (美國城市名)
2. stinky [ˋstɪŋkɪ] *adj.* 臭的
3. insult [ˋɪnsʌlt] *v.* 侮辱，羞辱
4. smelly [ˋsmɛlɪ] *adj.* 有臭味的
5. mislead [mɪsˋlid] *v.* 誤導

6. ambiguous [æmˋbɪgjuəs] *adj.* 模稜兩可的，模糊不清的
7. offensive [əˋfɛnsɪv] *adj.* 無禮的，冒犯的
8. judgmental [dʒʌdʒˋmɛntl̩] *adj.* 下判斷的
9. update [ʌpˋdet] *v.* (使情報、訊息等) 更新

Listening Practice

Listen to the following questions or statements, and choose the most appropriate responses.

_____ 1. (A) In six weeks.
(B) Six times a year.
(C) Two years from now.
(D) About three months ago.

_____ 2. (A) A good dictionary is worth buying.
(B) Yeah, you have to tell them apart by experience.
(C) There're a variety of dictionaries.
(D) The long story confused me a lot.

_____ 3. (A) Yap, she was mounting the platform.
(B) No, I have no glue in my tool box.
(C) Yap, she was reviewing chapter seven.
(D) No, she was falling into sleep then.

_____ 4. (A) Come on. Don't believe in rumors.
(B) That's right. My people are safe and sound.
(C) Okay, let's give it a try.
(D) Fine. Get whatever you want.

_____ 5. (A) You can call them on the cell phone.
(B) You may call them minority groups.
(C) You can't help calling them quite often.
(D) You may not call them in the face.

CONVERSATION II

Chris (C) and Sean (S) are looking around in the bookstore, and Laura (L) is coming their way.

L : Hi, boys. What're you doing here? That's really news to see you in the bookstore, son.

S : Good afternoon, Mrs. Parker. It's my pleasure to see you again. I'm Sean, Chris' friend.

C : Oh, Mom, what a ¹**coincidence**! You don't have to work this afternoon?

L : Well, I happened to pass by, getting the gifts I ordered. You two are looking for something?

C : Actually, Sean wants to get an updated dictionary to replace his old, ²**lousy** one.

S : I can't tell which English words may cause offense, so I don't know how to avoid using them.

C : That's true. This morning, Sean asked me something about "stinky Negroes" in the States!

L : Well, I see. Sean, please don't feel bad about your English. It's natural for people to make some cultural mistakes when using a language they're not familiar with. Chris is no exception when speaking ³**Mandarin**. Believe me. It takes time to get across the ⁴**bottleneck**.

C : Come on, Mom. It's not time to make me lose face. Can you give Sean any advice?

L : For me, when I have to talk to members of unfamiliar cultural groups, I always ask them which terms they prefer to be called. It's better to ask people than to risk ⁵**offending** them.

C : Oh, Mom, you're the most sensible woman on the planet!

L : You silly boy. Well, Sean, also, you should avoid using ⁶**slang** terms to refer to people, because many slang terms for people are insulting.

S : Mrs. Parker, thank you for giving me such good suggestions. They're very helpful.

L : You're welcome. Learning a language well is important, but it's more important to remember showing respect for different people. You two are good boys.

Words and Phrases

1. coincidence [ko`ɪnsɪdəns] *n.* 巧合
2. lousy [`laʊzɪ] *adj.*(俚語)糟糕的
3. Mandarin [`mændərɪn] *n.* 國語
4. bottleneck [`bɑtḷˌnɛk] *n.* 瓶頸(比喻難以突破之處)
5. offend [ə`fɛnd] *v.* 冒犯
6. slang [slæŋ] *n.* 俚語

Oral Practice

Part I: Blank-filling dialogues

❶A: Hi, Viola. What're you doing here? ░░░░░░░░░░░░░░░░░░░░░░░░░░░░ in the 3C mall.

B: Oh, Jeremy, ░░░░░░░░░░░░░░░░░░! You don't have to work in the afternoon?

A: Well, ░░░░░░░░░░░░░░░░░░░░░░░░░░░░░░, taking a glance around. You ░░░░░░░░░░░░░░░░░░░░ something?

B: ░░░░░░░░░░, I want to get an ░░░░░░░░░ laptop to ░░░░░░░░░ the old, ░░░░░░░░░░ one.

❷A: Louise, I can't tell how I should behave, so I don't know how to talk to the guests.

B: I see. Derek, please don't feel bad about that. ░░░░░░░░░░░░░░░░ people ░░░░░░░░░░░░░░░░░░░░░░░░░░░░░░ on an occasion ░░░░░░░░░░░░░░░░░ ░░░░░░░░░. I'm ░░░░░░░░░░░░░░░░░░░ when going to a new party. Believe me. It takes time to ░░░░░░░░░░░░░░░░░░░░░░░░░░.

Part II: Open discussions

❶Have you ever heard any impolite, offensive, or even insulting terms people use to refer to someone? How do you feel when hearing those terms?

❷What are possible reasons that people get used to using offensive terms to talk about someone in another identity group?

To Be PC or Not to Be PC?

You probably have heard somebody using words that made you feel uncomfortable.

For example, you are one of the physically challenged, and you have been called "a cripple." You mentioned you were going to see a professor, and then you heard a reply like this, "I hope you'll have a good talk with 'him'," even though you did not say whether the professor was a male, or a female.

To show respect for people, the improper and impolite expressions above should be [1]**substituted** in politically correct terms.

Politically correct language, also known as PC language, results from an attempt to use language without offending those in other different races, cultures, or identities. During the 1990s, being politically correct was a key issue in political and social policies. Later on, the trend spread into the mass media. From then on, using PC language has become mainstream in society.

However, there have been problems with using PC language by far. First of all, there is a [2]**blurring** line between PC or non-PC terms. In the States, while it is thought to be non-PC to refer to people in African origin as "black," yet many people in the group feel fine with the term instead of taking it as offensive.

In addition, some [3]**critics** say PC language may be [4]**overused** to such an [5]**extent**

that no expression can be made at all. One extreme example can be found in a humorous book on bedtime stories in PC language by James Finn Gardner: Cinderella has a "fairy godperson" instead of the classic "fairy godmother," and the seven " [6]**dwarfs**" in Snow White are called seven " [7]**vertically challenged** men."

Certainly, PC language has its great value in showing [8]**empathy** for those with different physical, mental, or racial conditions. Nevertheless, can the good-will choice be taken too far from reality?

This is an interesting but tricky question, and perhaps, only Cinderella's "fairy godperson" knows the answer best.

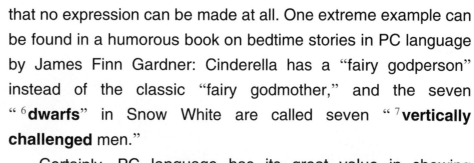

see WORD BANK FOR READINGS
page 160

Reading Comprehension

According to the passage on the left page, choose the most appropriate answers to the following questions.

_____ 1. What is the theme of the passage?

    (A) A language that helps people to offend others.

    (B) A problem already unsolved for a long time.

    (C) An effort to respect different people in language.

    (D) An attempt to speak language impolitely.

_____ 2. Which may be a non-PC term?

    (A) The physically challenged.　(B) A cripple.

    (C) She or he/Her or him.　(D) The vertically challenged.

_____ 3. What is the strong criticism against the use of PC language?

    (A) It makes speakers fall victim to political pressures.

    (B) It gives speakers too many terms to memorize.

    (C) It is too difficult to learn and too seldom to use.

    (D) It can be overused for speakers to express themselves clearly.

_____ 4. In the last paragraph, what does the author mean?

    (A) Cinderella's fairy person has the most powerful magic.

    (B) PC language can only be used in the fairy tale storybooks.

    (C) The use of PC language is still a question under discussion.

    (D) Lines in the books of PC terms are very blurring.

_____ 5. Which of the following statements is TRUE?

    (A) The term "Black" is not necessarily offensive to some people of African origin.

    (B) The mass media had nothing to do with the use of PC language.

    (C) People with different physical, mental, or racial conditions must use PC language.

    (D) Those words that make people uncomfortable are mostly in PC language.

Was It Something I Said?

Dear Eugene:

I'm writing to you because I really feel I fail to understand this country.

Everybody keeps telling me that the United States is a great place, but I've found people here are so cold and quite mean.

Last night, I went to the supermarket. A guy at the cash register looked short. I wanted to greet him by saying something interesting. So I said, "Hey, [1]**Shorty**! Do you need a ladder to reach the cash register?" Strangely enough, he didn't laugh but got mad, loudly asking me to get out of the store!

Later, when I took a walk down to the park, I saw an old woman sitting on the bench. I sat down beside her, and she told me I was very handsome. To be friendly, I decided to invite her to share her life experiences. So I said, "[2]**Oldie** Lady, how does it feel to live for so long? Will 100 years be enough?" To my surprise, the old woman got very angry, and told me to leave her alone!

What did I do wrong? Is this an unfriendly country, or what? Please help me.

Sincerely,

Milos

Dear Milos:

I can tell you were trying to be nice, and I know English seems not to be your mother tongue. Yet I've got to tell you your expressions are insulting to the people you talked to.

When talking about any of someone's differences, like physical features in your case, you should remember showing empathy and respect in the expressions you make.

If you stood in their shoes, you should know short people would never like to be reminded that they were not that tall. Similarly, the elderly wouldn't like to be told how old they were. Instead of [3]**commenting** on their height or age, you should have said hello and talked about something pleasant, yet less personal, like beautiful [4]**scenery**, or good TV programs.

Anyway, think twice before you say anything about somebody's differences. If you can do that, you'll find the country a warm and friendly place.

Yours truly,

Eugene

see WORD BANK FOR READINGS
page 160

Reading Comprehension

According to the passage on the left page, choose the most appropriate answers to the following questions.

_____ 1. What is the main purpose of Milos for writing to Eugene?

(A) Milos wants to talk about social problems in the country.

(B) Milos plans to discuss the secret that keeps him handsome.

(C) Milos means to tell a story about sales in different stores.

(D) Milos hopes to know what he did wrong.

_____ 2. Why does Milos use offensive terms in English?

(A) Milos is too nice and shy to talk with people naturally.

(B) English may not be a language Milos is good at.

(C) Milos cannot see how people are getting shorter or older.

(D) The country is an unfriendly place for anyone.

_____ 3. Why does Eugene ask Milos to "stand in one's shoes"?

(A) She wants him to be aware of the status of the people he talks to.

(B) She tells him that he cannot stand well if he is not wearing his shoes.

(C) She asks him to wear others' shoes even if they are not fitting.

(D) She advises him that he put on someone else's shoes to be taller.

_____ 4. Which is NOT one of the suggestions Eugene gives to Milos?

(A) Milos should show empathy and respect for people.

(B) Milos should avoid having eye contact with people.

(C) Milos should first say something pleasant to people.

(D) Milos should think more before he says anything about people.

_____ 5. Which of the following statements is FALSE?

(A) "Shorty" and "Oldie Lady" can be offensive, or even insulting.

(B) Milos is much confused about the way he speaks to people.

(C) Neither Milos nor Eugene thinks the country as a friendly place.

(D) Eugene shows empathy for Milos' mistake in using impolite terms.

[63] TOOTHPASTE, LAUNDRY SOAP, AND POLITICAL [2]CORRECTNESS

"An ancient Chinese secret [3]**resolves** all!" What is this commercial line about? Is it a book about [4]**herbal medicine**, or is it a [5]**gourmet** [6]**recipe**?

Sorry, it is a commercial line about laundry soap!

Are Chinese people famous for washing clothes? Of course not. However, in the earlier days, many Chinese owned dry cleaners in the States. That is why, when it comes to laundry soap, people only think about Chinese. That sounds stupid, right?

With a black man's face and his super white [7]**sparkling** teeth on the cover, what do you think the product may be? Yes, the product is a tube of toothpaste, with the brand name Darkie. Again, are all black people noted for extremely white teeth, or for being good dentists?

Obviously, the answer is "no" either. However, in the eye of many [8]**Asians**, black people do have [9]**shining** white teeth. Therefore, when the toothpaste was to be sold on the market, Asian [10]**advertisers** just took the image for [11]**marketing**.

In fact, many commercials represent [12]**irrational**, outdated stereotypes toward a specific race or an identity group. These commercials are convenient or humorous for some audience, but they are also offensive, and even insulting to the subjects in focus.

However, following the political and social trend, since the 1980s, advertisers have increasingly used politically correct language in commercials. [13]**Consequently**, instead of "blacks," "African Americans" are widely used. Darkie is replaced by Darlie. Chinese people have stopped selling any ancient secret for laundry soap.

Even so, it is not easy to sit back and relax now that advertisers seem to learn to speak in politically correct language. Some advertisers are still [14]**repeatedly** using non-PC tricks to sell their products in the mass media. Never get surprised if you have heard [15]**slogans** like "For a woman, the slimmer, the better," or "A man cannot be a real man without a macho look," on TV, over the radio, or on the Internet.

All in all, next time you happen to see commercials in the media, you can have a good chance to closely look at any possible stereotypes hidden behind them.

▷ see WORD BANK FOR READINGS
page 160

Reading Comprehension

According to the passage on the left page, choose the most appropriate answers to the following questions.

_____ 1. What is the topic of the passage?
   (A) Products that companies promote in their commercials.
   (B) Languages that advertisers use in their commercials.
   (C) Brands that companies represent in their commercials.
   (D) Races that advertisers mention in their commercials.

_____ 2. Which can PC advertisers do with their commercials?
   (A) They don't use the "Chinese-secret" way to sell laundry soap.
   (B) They put a black man with super white teeth on the cover of their products.
   (C) They imply that beautiful women should be all slim.
   (D) They refer to people of African origin as "blacks."

_____ 3. What kind of commercial can be inferred as a PC-advertised one?
   (A) A commercial that tells black people are good at selling toothpaste.
   (B) A commercial that use half naked women to sell computers.
   (C) A commercial that shows men and women can just be themselves.
   (D) A commercial that says only Chinese wash clothes clean enough.

_____ 4. Why is it still NOT easy for customers to relax about advertising slogans?
   (A) Today's advertising is impossible to understand.
   (B) Customers always have a close look at the mass media.
   (C) Advertisers focus on good images for marketing.
   (D) There are still old stereotypes used to promote products.

_____ 5. Which of the following statements is TRUE?
   (A) It is not Chinese but blacks that know the ancient secret.
   (B) Stereotypes are nowhere to be seen on the products.
   (C) Role images in commercials have changed with social trends.
   (D) Specific races or identity groups can be seen in many commercials.

Explaining Causes & Effects: Part II
解釋原因和結果（二）

1. 若使用解釋原因和結果的方法發展段落，有以下呈現補充細節的類型：

   a. 以原因為重心，之後檢視數個產生的結果。

   b. 以結果為重心，之後檢視數個形成的原因。

2. 使用解釋原因和結果的方法時，可在說明的論點之前適當使用適當轉接詞 (transitional words)，協助讀者了解事件具有原因或產生結果的部分：

   a. 表示「原因」時，可用 because, because of, on account of, due to 等。

   b. 表示「結果」時，可用 so, therefore, as a result, consequently 等。

Drills: In each of the following paragraphs, separately mark out its main idea and causes or effects for explaining and, if any, highlight the transitional words.

1. Many commercials represent outdated stereotypical images people have toward a certain race, culture, or other specific groups. However, because of influences of the political trends, since 1980s, advertisers have come to use more politically correct language. Consequently, instead of "black," the term "African-American" has been widely used.

2. On account of an attempt to use less offensive language, there exists politically correct language, also known as PC language. During the 1990s, being politically correct became a hot issue in U.S. national policies, so the trend spread over the mass media. As a result, properly using PC terms and expressions has been popular.

3. It is likely to have sunstroke due to exposure to the sunlight for too long. Sunstroke often causes great pain, such as headache and fever. The situation can be worse when a person with sunstroke passes out. It is noteworthy that serious or prolonged sunstroke can even bring about permanent damage to the human body.

Proper Use of Politically Correct (PC) Terms
適當使用政治正確的用語

1. 使用政治正確用語的目的是：為了表示尊重(respect)，在指稱某個特定種族、文化等類型群體(identity group)時，用字遣詞應盡可能的減少冒犯(minimize offense)。

2. 使用政治正確用語的準則是：在描述個人或某團體時，避免使用帶有評判語氣的 (judgmental)或是具有歧視意味的(discriminatory)字句，而是使用客觀的(objective)和中立的(neutral)措詞。

3. 由於寫作是正式的語文表達，在指稱特定主體(subject)時，應格外注意適當使用政治正確用語。

Drills: The list below provides several generally seen non-PC words. Find out their corresponding PC terms and meanings.

Field	Non-PC Word	PC Term	Meaning
Gender	1. mankind [U]		
	2. manpower [U]		
	3. businessman		
	4. fireman		
	5. policeman		
	6. stewardess		
Racial and Ethnic Groups	1. black		
	2. oriental		
	3. American Indian		
Illness & Disability	1. AIDS victims		
	2. mental patients		
	3. the handicapped		
	4. the retarded		
	5. the blind/deaf		
Age	old, elderly		
Sexuality	gay/lesbian		
Physical Traits	1. fat		
	2. skinny		

聽力測驗

🎧⁸ 簡短對話：本部分共 5 題，請於聽到播出的一段對話及一個相關的問題之後，從以下各題之 A、B、C、D 四個選項中，選出一個最適合的回答。每題只播出一次。

1. (A) The discount on a holiday trip.
   (B) The wonders on the way to Hawaii.
   (C) Their feelings about a vacation trip.
   (D) Preventions against possible disasters.

2. (A) In a bank.
   (B) On campus.
   (C) In a museum.
   (D) On board.

3. (A) When they ride a motorcycle.
   (B) When they have candlelight dinner.
   (C) When they walk around together.
   (D) When they see a movie.

4. (A) He speaks patiently.
   (B) He speaks angrily.
   (C) He speaks sadly.
   (D) He speaks indifferently.

5. (A) He'll feed his pet birds.
   (B) He'll call his friend for dinner.
   (C) He'll swim in the pool.
   (D) He'll go buy necessary outfits.

閱讀能力測驗

一、詞彙與結構：本部份共5題，每題含1個空格。請從以下各題之A、B、C、D四個選項中，選出最適合題意的字詞。

_____ 1. If you can _____ other people around, that means you've grown up.
(A) blush
(B) protect
(C) contrast
(D) involve

_____ 2. Using proper words and phrases in the textbook _____ important.
(A) were having
(B) have been
(C) is
(D) are

_____ 3. Simon seems to have great _____ for the volunteer work he is doing.
(A) participants
(B) affections
(C) sponsors
(D) intimacy

_____ 4. No one can stop me _____ forward on my journey in life.
(A) despite
(B) regardless of
(C) so as to
(D) from moving

_____ 5. It is really a _____ problem to settle down the refugees in the country.
(A) complicated
(B) opposite
(C) physical
(D) inappropriate

二、段落填空：本部份共5題，分別為以下段落中的5個空格。請從以下各題之A、B、C、D四個選項中，選出最適合題意的字詞。

Until he turned 30, Jass Patel, a British Indian, only dated white women. When he thought of Indian women, he thought of ___6___ marriages that bother him. ___7___, now that Jass gets older, he thinks that marrying someone from his own culture might not be a bad idea.

His experience shows that though cross-cultural dating has become more common in Britain, a person's cultural ___8___ still plays an important role when deciding whom to marry. Most white people in Britain view dating and marrying as ___9___ decisions. Though factors as class and religion are important, people are free to date ___10___ they like. Both men and women usually date many different people before choosing a mate.

_____ 6. (A) appeared
(B) arranged
(C) appealed
(D) appreciated

_____ 7. (A) Otherwise
(B) Besides
(C) Therefore
(D) However

_____ 8. (A) battlefield
(B) background
(C) guidelines
(D) crossroads

_____ 9. (A) ignorant
(B) collaborative
(C) individual
(D) improving

_____ 10. (A) whomever
(B) however
(C) wherever
(D) whenever

三、閱讀理解：本部分共5題，包含一段短文，後有5個相關問題。請從以下各題之A、B、C、D四個選項中，選出最適合題意的答案。

Internet dating has gone from daring to dull. As a result, many singles these days are looking to their cell phones instead of their laptops in an effort to locate love.

Cell phone technology now allows users to post tiny photographs and mini-profiles to a dating service mailbox, which can be visited by other cell users in search of a date. When a profile looks promising, users use their phones to send a text message to their person of interest.

Some phone dating services also are experimenting with ways to turn cell phones into homing devices. In other words, the phones can alert users to potential dates who may be just a short distance away—or, at the other end of the bar.

Europeans are heavily into phone dating, and China, which has 430 million cell phone users, also has embraced "mobile romance."

The wireless service providers love phone dating, too, because all that text messaging pumps up their revenues. Analysts estimate that global mobile dating revenues were US$31 million in 2005; by 2009, that figure is projected to reach US$215 million.

Some people say that phone dating is more about flirting than about serious romance. "People who want to use their mobile devices are more interested in shorter-term relationships than people who want to use their computer," said an officer of Match.com, a service with a quarter-million mobile users.

But, who really can say for sure. The next time the cell phone rings, it could be one calling from Cupid.

____ 11. How can someone get information on any possible date on the cell p hone?
　　　(A) By asking the operator.
　　　(B) By making an emergency call.
　　　(C) By using a laptop.
　　　(D) By looking at mini-photos in dating mailbox.

____ 12. Which is the function the dating service can offer through cell phones?
　　　(A) Increasing user's revenues.　　　(B) Alerting users to potential dates.
　　　(C) Holding a wedding.　　　(D) Giving a gift to possible dates.

____ 13. Who may gain the most advantage of cell phone dating economically?
　　　(A) Users.　　　(B) Possible dates.
　　　(C) The wireless service suppliers.　　　(D) The store owners.

14. What are cell phone romance seekers often interested in?
   (A) Getting a new laptop.　　　　　(B) Shorter-term relationships.
   (C) Finding other phone users.　　　(D) Short distance callings.

15. What can be the best title for the passage?
   (A) Cupid's Cell Phone Calls　　　　(B) A Very Special Date
   (C) New Laptops, New Cell Phones　　(D) Fun of Online Dating

寫作能力測驗

一、中譯英：請將下列的一段中文翻譯成通順、達意且前後連貫的英文。

　　每個人在遇到自己喜歡的人時，總會想辦法讓彼此有機會更接近。約會就是進一步認識彼此最好的方法之一。

二、英文作文：請依以下的提示寫一篇英文作文，長度約120字(8至12個句子)。(評分重點包括內容、組織、文法、用字、標點、大小寫)。

提示：英語早已成為世界共通的語言之一了。請以你自己的經驗為例，說明學習英語的重要。

聽力測驗

🎧 簡短對話：本部分共 5 題，請於聽到播出的一段對話及一個相關的問題之後，從以下各題之 A、B、C、D 四個選項中，選出一個最適合的回答。每題只播出一次。

1. (A) To the clinic.
   (B) To the kindergarten.
   (C) To the railway station.
   (D) To the church.

2. (A) About some handsome men.
   (B) About wearing uniforms.
   (C) About summer vacation.
   (D) About nylon umbrellas.

3. (A) It's pleasant.
   (B) It's embarrassing.
   (C) It's confusing.
   (D) It's exhausting.

4. (A) She escapes.
   (B) She accepts.
   (C) She vanishes.
   (D) She disagrees.

5. (A) The man wants to be a cook.
   (B) The woman has a good cook book.
   (C) The man doesn't like cooking.
   (D) The woman bought a good cooker.

閱讀能力測驗

一、 詞彙與結構：本部份共5題，每題含1個空格。請從以下各題之A、B、C、D四個選項中，選出最適合題意的字詞。

_____ 1. The candidate's policies are not [   ] at all; instead, they are quite reserved.

(A) liberal　　　　(B) powerful　　　　(C) fearless　　　　(D) remarkable

_____ 2. Tea [   ] an important drink to Chinese for thousands of years.

(A) had been　　　(B) has been　　　　(C) to have been　　(D) having been

_____ 3. Finally, he will know it is stupid to [   ] his free time for fame and fortune.

(A) trade　　　　(B) participate　　　(C) consider　　　　(D) dominate

_____ 4. The report proves the theory [   ] false and incorrect.

(A) as　　　　　　(B) in　　　　　　　(C) to be　　　　　(D) to have

_____ 5. The warrior s knew the [   ] will belong to them in the end of the war.

(A) vehicle　　　　(B) viewpoint　　　(C) voter　　　　　(D) victory

二、 段落填空：本部份共5題，分別為以下段落中的5個空格。請從以下各題之A、B、C、D四個選項中，選出最適合題意的字詞。

"If employees can spend enough time with their families, they will do better work for the company." ____6____ this idea, our company offers six months of paid time off to new mothers and fathers. Mothers almost always take the time off to rest and care for their children, but I've found fathers rarely take ____7____ of this benefit.

Employers' attitudes toward family are changing, but employees, men and women, do not ____8____. Many men still believe only women should care for children. ____9____ mothers have a physical bond with their babies, fathers have no traditional models of child-caring. To add to the difficulty, men are afraid if they leave their jobs for too long, they may be passed over for a ____10____ or looked upon negatively by their boss or co-workers.

_____ 6. (A) To support　　(B) To supporting　　(C) Supported　　(D) Support

_____ 7. (A) participation　(B) battlefield　　　(C) advantage　　(D) contribution

_____ 8. (A) adapt　　　　(B) adept　　　　　(C) adopt　　　　(D) adequate

_____ 9. (A) So　　　　　(B) While　　　　　(C) Unless　　　　(D) And

10. (A) efforts　　　(B) poverty　　　(C) election　　　(D) promotion

三、閱讀理解：本部分共5題，包含一段短文，後有5個相關問題。請從以下各題之A、B、C、D四個選項中，選出最適合題意的答案。

Japan is still, in many respects, a very traditional society. Men wear a suit and a tie and go to work in the office, while women remain at home and care for the children.

Recently, though, Japanese women have been quietly changing. By trading foreign currencies on their computers at home while their husbands are at work, they have been able to earn money on their own.

An entire female culture of currency trading has developed in Japan. There are television programs, books, and even manga comics based on it. Clubs have been formed in which the women meet to exchange knowledge and advice.

The foreign exchange markets have been dramatically affected by the housewives' activity. Each day, these women trade around US$9 billion worth of currency. This is about one fifth of the total global currency trading during Japanese office hours.

Some of the women made huge amounts of money. One Japanese housewife was even arrested because she had failed to pay US$1 million in taxes on the profits she had made.

Mostly, the women had been betting that the Yen would fall. For a long time, it did and they made lots of money. Recently, though, the foreign exchange markets have become more changeable. The Yen started to rise again, and many women lost all of the money they had earned. Anyway, the trading has allowed women at home to achieve financial success as well.

11. What can be the best title for the passage?
    (A) Spending of Japanese Housewives
    (B) Japanese Women in the Office
    (C) Japanese Housewives Shake the World
    (D) Why Women Worry?

12. By which means do the housewives in Japan earn huge money?
    (A) By trading foreign currencies on computers.
    (B) By selling homemade products.
    (C) By working with their husbands.
    (D) By watching TV programs.

13. Why is there an entire female culture of currency trading in Japan?

(A) The government gives an order.

(B) The market of the group is huge.

(C) The books and manga comics read so.

(D) The foreign exchange is closed.

14. How much do the women in Japan affect the foreign exchange market every day?

(A) US$9 billion.　　　　(B) US$1 million.

(C) Two fifth of the total.　　　　(D) One seventh of the total.

15. For what reason do the Japanese women earn a large amount of money?

(A) They bet US dollars rise.　　　　(B) They bet US dollars fall.

(C) They bet Yen rises.　　　　(D) They bet Yen falls.

寫作能力測驗

一、中譯英：請將下列的一段中文翻譯成通順、達意且前後連貫的英文。

以前男性被認為不能輕易哭泣，而女性則被認為不能強悍。但是，隨著時代的進步，每個人都應有選擇自己內心性別 (gender) 的權利，勇敢的做自己。

二、英文作文：請依以下的提示寫一篇英文作文，長度約120字(8至12個句子)。(評分重點包括內容、組織、文法、用字、標點、大小寫)。

提示：學生們總是喜歡沒事就「掛」在網路上 (get hooked on the Internet)。請舉例說明造成此現象的原因。

聽力測驗

簡短對話：本部分共 5 題，請於聽到播出的一段對話及一個相關的問題之後，從以下各題之 A、B、C、D 四個選項中，選出一個最適合的回答。每題只播出一次。

1. (A) He feels doubtful.
   (B) He feels disappointed.
   (C) He feels frightened
   (D) He feels confident.

2. (A) She'll do her assignments.
   (B) She'll make other people know about her.
   (C) She'll protect her skin.
   (D) She'll raise a pet.

3. (A) He needs many pies.
   (B) He needs a good apartment.
   (C) He needs much information.
   (D) He needs a high salary.

4. (A) He's a librarian.
   (B) He's a salesperson.
   (C) He's an engineer.
   (D) He's a freelancer.

5. (A) Her home is too large and too noisy.
   (B) She may get no customers.
   (C) She always mixes work with home life.
   (D) She's got nobody to have a talk with.

閱讀能力測驗

一、 詞彙與結構：本部份共5題，每題含1個空格。請從以下各題之A、B、C、D四個選項中，選出最適合題意的字詞。

_____ 1. Her excellent speech really ▨▨▨▨ the audience to take action for human rights.
(A) implied   (B) increased   (C) inspired   (D) included

_____ 2. A grasshopper, ▨▨▨▨ the name suggests, is an insect always hopping on the grass.
(A) that   (B) on   (C) which   (D) as

_____ 3. With the development of the area, the housing business becomes ▨▨▨▨ again.
(A) exotic   (B) conventional   (C) profitable   (D) irregular

_____ 4. Smoking too much not only costs much ▨▨▨▨ harms health.
(A) but   (B) and   (C) unless   (D) until

_____ 5. There are much more ▨▨▨▨ in the city than in the country.
(A) candidates   (B) distractions   (C) conferences   (D) statistics

二、 段落填空：本部份共5題，分別為以下段落中的5個空格。請從以下各題之A、B、C、D四個選項中，選出最適合題意的字詞。

I __6__ SOHO working at just the right time. SOHO is a new working style that entirely takes place at home or in a small office. I decided to leave my regular job and start working as a freelance editor from home. Many women find SOHO jobs __7__ them the freedom to choose when to work. SOHO jobs also give women the __8__ to stay in the workforce while raising their children.

__9__ the benefits, it's still challenging to balance my freelance jobs with child-raising. I would caution other women to avoid working double-time __10__ sure their spouses put in an equal share. Make your SOHO jobs work around your schedule, and you may begin to set a healthier and more enjoyable pace of life.

_____ 6. (A) disconnected   (B) disagreed   (C) disappeared   (D) discovered
_____ 7. (A) give   (B) giving   (C) to give   (D) given
_____ 8. (A) fee   (B) impatience   (C) department   (D) opportunity
_____ 9. (A) Despite   (B) Among   (C) Into   (D) By
_____ 10. (A) for giving   (B) in letting   (C) by making   (D) to cutting

三、閱讀理解：本部分共5題，包含一段短文，後有5個相關問題。請從以下各題之A、B、
C、D四個選項中，選出最適合題意的答案。

In Tainan, milkfish has been central to people's diets for many years. In 2004, it occurred to Lu Su-feng, a 35-year-old mother of three, that this food could do more than feed her. It could provide a successful business. So with some hard work, she turned her idea into a reality.

Ms. Lu had the imaginative ideas of using milkfish to make hamburgers, hot dogs, and, believe it or not, popsicles. Once she learned some basic knowledge of Internet use, she created a business that brings in NT$100,000 a month. Best of all, as transactions are done on the Internet, she has a flexible schedule to look after her family.

Ms. Lu experienced some common problems when women try to create thier own business. According to a study by the National Youth Commission, 27% of women do not have the professional skills to start a business, and 22% do not have the start-up money. Most surprisingly, 12% of women say they are unable to run a business.

Ms. Lu's road to success was difficult. Plus, she still must maintain a balance between the needs of work and family life. But her story can serve as an inspiration for women who want to make it in the business world.

_____ 11. Why did milkfish mean so much to Ms. Lu?

(A) It became tasteless on the table. (B) It helped her build up a career.

(C) It looked beautiful in the pond. (D) It all got caught in Tainan.

_____ 12. What did Ms. Lu do with milkfish?

(A) She made it meet her family.

(B) She posted its picture.

(C) She sold it in the department store.

(D) She got it cooked into various dishes.

_____ 13. Which is NOT one of the difficulties for women to create a business of their own?

(A) Having no sense of duty. (B) Having no confidence.

(C) Having no money to start. (D) Having no professional skills.

_____ 14. What is the author's comment on Lu's example?

(A) It is countless. (B) It is a disaster.

(C) It is basic. (D) It is inspiring anyhow.

15. What may be the most appropriate title for the passage?
    (A) Life Span of Milkfish
    (B) Figures on Working Attitudes
    (C) Women Fighting for Business of Their Own
    (D) Family Bonds

寫作能力測驗

一、中譯英：請將下列的一段中文翻譯成通順、達意且前後連貫的英文。

　　由於無線網路與筆記型電腦的便利，現代人的工作地點已經不限定在辦公室。許多人享有選擇自己喜愛工作場合的自由，加入 SOHO 族的行列。

二、英文作文：請依以下的提示寫一篇英文作文，長度約120字(8至12個句子)。(評分重點包括內容、組織、文法、用字、標點、大小寫)。

提示：現代人生活忙碌，適時的休息和放鬆顯得格外重要。請討論利用短短幾分鐘時間讓自己休息放鬆的步驟。

聽力測驗

簡短對話：本部分共 5 題，請於聽到播出的一段對話及一個相關的問題之後，從以下各題之 A、B、C、D 四個選項中，選出一個最適合的回答。每題只播出一次。

1. (A) When the man can write the report.
   (B) When the man may have time for her.
   (C) When the man will ride the horse.
   (D) When the man can get rid of her.

2. (A) He'll buy a new disk in the display.
   (B) He'll crash the computer on his desk.
   (C) He'll learn the way to surf the Internet.
   (D) He'll click the mouse and shut down the screen.

3. (A) They're taking a rest.
   (B) They're practicing singing.
   (C) They're seeing a doctor.
   (D) They're taking photographs.

4. (A) She disappoints him by lying.
   (B) She deprives him of his freedom.
   (C) She disagrees on his act.
   (D) She delivers a false message to him.

5. (A) He feels unpleased with her question.
   (B) He feels thrilled to hear her question.
   (C) He feels her question is quite fair.
   (D) He feels there's an error in her question sentence.

閱讀能力測驗

一、詞彙與結構：本部份共5題，每題含1個空格。請從以下各題之A、B、C、D四個選項中，選出最適合題意的字詞。

_____ 1. John will possibly be _____ if he is unable to do the task.
   (A) captured   (B) replaced   (C) struck   (D) located

_____ 2. More than one singer _____ ever sung the beautiful song.
   (A) has   (B) have   (C) had   (D) having

_____ 3. Please don't worry. We can discuss the problem in _____.
   (A) sensational   (B) handsome   (C) crazed   (D) private

_____ 4. Without a strong governemnt, human society _____ collapse in no time.
   (A) has   (B) need   (C) dare   (D) would

_____ 5. Prof. Car briefly introduced the _____ in this chapter and then offered details.
   (A) tabloids   (B) presentation   (C) subjects   (D) scandals

二、段落填空：本部份共5題，分別為以下段落中的5個空格。請從以下各題之A、B、C、D四個選項中，選出最適合題意的字詞。

I'm a paparazzi photographer and I make my living by taking photographs of the world's most famous people. I won't argue there are ___6___ in the job, ___7___ the celebrities I follow around can make my work a real nightmare.

Imagine how hard it is to track down an actress when she is trying hard to avoid me. I have to spend months ___8___ out where she shops, goes out for dinner and takes her vacations. There'll be finally one moment when she will do something interesting. If I get lucky, catching the actress go sunbathing in the arms of a ___9___ man on a private beach, the photograph ___10___ in a magazine.

_____ 6. (A) borders   (B) benefits   (C) buzz   (D) bodyguards
_____ 7. (A) that   (B) until   (C) and   (D) but
_____ 8. (A) find   (B) to find   (C) finding   (D) found
_____ 9. (A) mysterious   (B) numerous   (C) handmade   (D) newborn
_____ 10. (A) to publish   (B) is publishing   (C) will be published (D) had published

三、 閱讀理解：本部分共5題，包含一段短文，後有5個相關問題。請從以下各題之A、B、C、D四個選項中，選出最適合題意的答案。

Life seems so easy for celebrities. They dine in fine restaurants, wear designer clothes, and have jobs such as acting or singing. It is just not fair for an ordinary man like me.

Luckily, God created the paparazzi to make these celebrities' lives a little bit challenging — They follow celebrities around town and do anything they can to snap a picture. As films and TV shows grow in popularity, more and more paparazzi begin appearing in the real life. They use secret cameras, hide in bushes, and even wear disguises to get a good photo.

In one case, one said he was in Michael Douglas' family so he could sneak in the hospital and snap a photo of his new baby. Sean Penn became a favorite target for the paparazzi because of his bad temper. Many paparazzi even tried to make Penn angry so they could get a more interesting picture.

After the death of Princess Diana, many countries began passing laws to limit the paparazzi and protect the privacy of celebrities. Are the paparazzi out of line or should celebrities accept these stalkers as a small price to pay for fame and fortune?

_____ 11. What is the author's attitude toward the celebrities' lifestyles?
    (A) The author feels regret for them.   (B) The author looks down on them.
    (C) The author gets mad at them.   (D) The author shows respect for them.

_____ 12. How does the author think of the effects of the paparazzi on celebrities' life?
    (A) They love it at heart.   (B) They have it painted.
    (C) They turn it into real.   (D) They make it difficult.

_____ 13. Which is NOT one of the tricks the paparazzi use to shoot good photos?
    (A) Giving a welcome party.   (B) Carrying a secret camera.
    (C) Hiding in bushes.   (D) Wearing disguises.

_____ 14. According to the passage, which of the following statements is NOT true ?
    (A) The more anger Sean Pam is, the more popular he is with the paparazzi.
    (B) Celebrities live a more miserable life than the paparazzi.
    (C) Privacy laws against the paparazzi were passed after Princess Diana's death.
    (D) One of the paparazzi pretended to be Michael Douglas's family to take picture of his new baby.

15. What may be the best title for the passage?

    (A) Safety Counts   (B) Stars in Luxury

    (C) Growth of Films and TV Shows   (D) Prices for Fame and Fortune

寫作能力測驗

中譯英：請將下列的一段中文翻譯成通順、達意且前後連貫的英文。

> 　　狗仔隊 (The paparazzi) 通常在名流 (celebrities) 出現的地方等候，並且準備偷拍。有時，他們貼身跟蹤目標的車輛，以求揭露名人不為人知的習慣及喜好。

英文作文：請依以下的提示寫一篇英文作文，長度約120字(8至12個句子)。(評分重點包括內容、組織、文法、用字、標點、大小寫)。

> 提示：作報告是每個學生必定有過的經驗。請以你曾經作的報告為例，說明你完成該報告的步驟。

聽力測驗

🎧 **40** 簡短對話：本部分共 5 題，請於聽到播出的一段對話及一個相關的問題之後，從以下各題之 A、B、C、D 四個選項中，選出一個最適合的回答。每題只播出一次。

1. (A) To make an introduction of Prof. Stone.
   (B) To do a course planning.
   (C) To meet Prof. Stone's needs.
   (D) To drop the course.

2. (A) The inner personalities of two students.
   (B) The academic performances of two students.
   (C) The important meeting of two students.
   (D) The accidental conflict of two students.

3. (A) They'll buy books for Ms. Chen.
   (B) They'll run away with Ms. Chen.
   (C) They'll go to Ms. Chen's office.
   (D) They'll shout at Ms. Chen.

4. (A) The man says something bad about her.
   (B) The man does nothing but complain to her.
   (C) The man forgets to say thanks to her.
   (D) The man remains silent all the time.

5. (A) They're classmates in the same class.
   (B) They're colleagues in the same office.
   (C) They're neighbors in the same building.
   (D) They're players in the same team.

閱讀能力測驗

一、 詞彙與結構：本部份共5題，每題含1個空格。請從以下各題之A、B、C、D四個選項中，選出最適合題意的字詞。

_____ 1. Nowadays, there's always _____ development in technology changing the way human society works.

    (A) disorderly   (B) innovative   (C) voluntary   (D) pregnant

_____ 2. Heavy rain is the main reason _____ the crops are seriously damaged.

    (A) which   (B) what   (C) why   (D) whom

_____ 3. At the end of the semester, your _____ to class will be included as part of evaluation.

    (A) forerunner   (B) attendance   (C) instillation   (D) experience

_____ 4. _____ is proven that global warming has been getting much worse by now.

    (A) What   (B) Who   (C) Which   (D) It

_____ 5. When you get into a new environment, try to _____ to it as much as possible.

    (A) admire   (B) educate   (C) adjust   (D) produce

二、 段落填空：本部份共5題，分別為以下段落中的5個空格。請從以下各題之A、B、C、D四個選項中，選出最適合題意的字詞。

In Tu Hsiu-hui's class, students who misbehave need not worry about corporal punishment. __6__, they must be ready to think about their action. Tu is one of the teachers in Taiwan who __7__ alternative methods to help students learn. She hopes students will show more concerns for others by thinking about the effects of their action.

__8__ teachers such as Tu, alternative teaching methods are becoming more common in Taiwan. Tu punishes her students by making them talk to each other, because she does not believe hitting students __9__ the real problems behind their actions. Many teachers in Taiwan now agree with Tu that __10__ strict teaching techniques work better.

_____ 6. (A) Besides   (B) Certainly   (C) Instead   (D) Later

_____ 7. (A) use   (B) to use   (C) using   (D) used

_____ 8. (A) Compared to   (B) Opposite to   (C) Thanks to   (D) Close to

_____ 9. (A) releases   (B) constructs   (C) disappears   (D) addresses

_____ 10. (A) little　　　　　(B) less　　　　　(C) few　　　　　(D) more

三、 閱讀理解：本部分共5題，包含一段短文，後有5 個相關問題。請從以下各題之A、B、
　　　C、D四個選項中，選出最適合題意的答案。

　In 1990, Pamela Smart was a teacher in a small American town, but she had a big dream—she wanted to be a star. Unfortunately, she thought her husband stood in her way. Then there came a sensational murder trial that featured today's soap opera—drugs, sex and rock'n'roll.

　Pamela Smart was just 22 when she met 15-year-old Billy Flynn at a drug-awareness program. She liked Billy's long hair and shared his passions for heavy metal bands. It wasn't long before the two were sharing more than music. Pamela began telling her young lover about her husband's problem. Divorce was impossible, she said—she'd lose everything. Greg Smart beat her, too, she claimed, which was untrue.

　She asked Billy to kill him. Billy obliged, and, with two friends, shot her husband to death. Pamela had an alibi for the time of the murder—she was at a meeting.

　However, police were suspicious. One noticed that Pamela called her dead husband "the body." Another saw her coldly walk through Greg's blood on the carpet. Police soon got confessions from the young murderers, who immediately implicated the teacher. Pamela said she was innocent, but the jury disagreed. She is still serving her jail time.

　Two movies subsequently were made about the case. One is the 1995 film "To Die For," staring Nicole Kidman in the leading role. It was just the kind of media attention that Pamela Smart had been willing to die for.

_____ 11. What is the passage mainly about?

(A) A murder.　　　(B) A movie star.　　　(C) A meeting.　　　(D) A trial.

_____ 12. How did the police view Pamela Smart's alibi?

(A) They made it.　　　　　　　　(B) They watched it.

(C) They disbelieved it.　　　　　　(D) They googled it.

_____ 13. How did Pamela Smart describe her husband to her younger lover?

(A) He cherished her.　　　　　　(B) He left her.

(C) He hit her.　　　　　　　　　(D) He held her.

14. What did Smart's young lover and his friends say about the case?

    (A) They enjoyed killing her husband.

    (B) They pointed her out as the planner.

    (C) They thought she was innocent.

    (D) They laughed at the case trial.

15. Which can be the best title of the passage?

    (A) An Ironic Dream   (B) A Stupid Husband

    (C) Attention to Die for   (D) Passions for Young Men

寫作能力測驗

一、 中譯英：請將下列的一段中文翻譯成通順、達意且前後連貫的英文。

從小學開始，我們受教於不同類型的老師。有些老師很嚴格，相對地有些老師很溫和。不同老師有不同的教學風格，但是，只要是位認真的老師，都值得學生尊敬。

二、 英文作文：請依以下的提示寫一篇英文作文，長度約120字(8至12個句子)。(評分重點包括內容、組織、文法、用字、標點、大小寫)。

提示：人生中，一定會有些事情對你影響很大。請敘述一個你認為對你影響最大的經驗，並且說明在這件事發生之前你的態度，及之後你的改變。

聽力測驗

🎧 **48** 簡短對話：本部分共 5 題，請於聽到播出的一段對話及一個相關的問題之後，從以下各題之 A、B、C、D 四個選項中，選出一個最適合的回答。每題只播出一次。

1. (A) Sam is difficult to get along with.
   (B) Sam is easy to control.
   (C) Sam is good in general.
   (D) Sam is hard to imagine.

2. (A) To wait for the concert tickets.
   (B) To stop giving big surprises.
   (C) To play the card game together.
   (D) To be Daphne's partner.

3. (A) To find Eason to have a talk.
   (B) To push Eason to trust him.
   (C) To betray Eason in return.
   (D) To help Eason to clean up.

4. (A) He'll look over the reference book about the question.
   (B) He'll give himself up to the question.
   (C) He'll keep himself quiet down over the question.
   (D) He'll ask the woman again to answer the question.

5. (A) About drawing a lot.
   (B) About giving a speech.
   (C) About writing a play.
   (D) About flying a kite.

閱讀能力測驗

一、詞彙與結構：本部份共5題，每題含1個空格。請從以下各題之A、B、C、D四個選項中，選出最適合題意的字詞。

_____ 1. The soldiers _____ to survive the cruel battlefield.
(A) triggered   (B) recognized   (C) witnessed   (D) struggled

_____ 2. If the experiment _____, the company will suffer great loss.
(A) will fail   (B) fails   (C) to fail   (D) failed

_____ 3. The bad news has not been _____ announced by the government.
(A) annually   (B) harshly   (C) officially   (D) brutally

_____ 4. Even on the holiday _____ people do not go to work, Casper still stays in the office.
(A) which   (B) when   (C) what   (D) why

_____ 5. Don't tell Irene. We're going to give her an _____ surprise.
(A) unexpected   (B) automatic   (C) international   (D) abroad

二、段落填空：本部份共5題，分別為以下段落中的5個空格。請從以下各題之A、B、C、D四個選項中，選出最適合題意的字詞。

When Chou Shang-hua married her partner in 2000, the two women enjoyed a service ___6___ by their family and friends. While they were lucky to be surrounded by people they love, they still did not feel entirely complete. As a same-sex couple in Taiwan, their marriage was not recognized ___7___ legal.

Chou and her partner were ___8___ thankful that their family and friends believed in their right to marry. In fact, 75% of Taiwanese adults now say that same-sex marriage should be legal, but it has still not been ___9___ by the government. As in many countries, conservatives are the main opponents, ___10___ that they want to defend "traditional" marriage.

_____ 6. (A) support   (B) to support   (C) supporting   (D) supported
_____ 7. (A) in   (B) to   (C) as   (D) at
_____ 8. (A) doubtfully   (B) especially   (C) partly   (D) mindlessly
_____ 9. (A) approved   (B) terrified   (C) confused   (D) stirred
_____ 10. (A) state   (B) to state   (C) stating   (D) stated

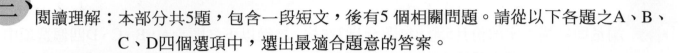

三、 閱讀理解：本部分共5題，包含一段短文，後有5個相關問題。請從以下各題之A、B、C、D四個選項中，選出最適合題意的答案。

Gay pride events have now become common. Almost every large city has one of its own each year. Colorful and musical, they have become tourist attractions, appreciated even by those who are not gay.

Not many people know the dark history that lies behind gay pride events, though. The truth is that when they first began, gay pride events were a symbol of anger rather than joy.

The first gay pride parades took place in America in the 1970s. Gay people were tired of the way they had been treated. No longer willing to hide, they wanted to live openly and fearlessly.

The passion that lay behind the original gay pride parades can be seen in their names. They were not called "gay pride" but "gay freedom" or "gay liberation" events and formed part of a powerful movement for social change.

Eventually, most cultures did change. They became more accepting of gay people. Then the gay parades became celebrations rather than displays of anger.

Unfortunately, until today, gay rights do not yet exist everywhere. In many countries in Eastern Europe, for example, gay pride parades have been greeted by violence. The mayor of Moscow, the capital city of Russia, has banned gay pride parades in the city and has spoken out against gay culture.

So, although the struggle to achieve equal rights for gay people has come this far, there is clearly still a long way to go.

_____ 11. What can be the best title for the passage?

(A) Violence Against Gays   (B) Gays in Great Danger

(C) Gay Parades Now and Then   (D) Let's Have Joys to Be Gay

_____ 12. Which of the following may NOT be part of gay parade nowadays?

(A) Fatal weapons.   (B) Colorful banners.

(C) Many tourists.   (D) Big celebrations.

_____ 13. Why were gay parades called "gay freedom" or "gay liberation" in earlier days?

(A) The names sounded clearer.   (B) The names presented attraction.

(C) The names are full of fears.   (D) The names showed their purposes.

_____ 14. What was something negative that happened to the gay parades in Moscow ?
(A) They were appreciated.
(B) They were viewed as common activities.
(C) They were taken as tourist spots.
(D) They were banned from being held.

_____ 15. What is the author's conclusion of the passage?
(A) Gay parades have gone too far.
(B) Gay people still have to fight for their rights.
(C) Gay campaigns ruin social change.
(D) Gays always walk very long.

寫作能力測驗

一、中譯英：請將下列的一段中文翻譯成通順、達意且前後連貫的英文。

　　事實上，就和其他所有人一樣，男同志 (gays) 和女同志 (lesbians) 也應該擁有生活空間和基本權利，以及親密甜美的伴侶關係。

二、英文作文：請依以下的提示寫一篇英文作文，長度約120字(8至12個句子)。(評分重點包括內容、組織、文法、用字、標點、大小寫)。

提示：雖然目前已經是網際網路 (Internet) 通行的世紀了，但是如報紙、雜誌、書籍等平面媒體 (print media) 仍然在生活中佔了很大的比重。請討論從平面媒體上和從網路上獲取資訊的方式，有什麼樣的相異點。

聽力測驗

🎧 簡短對話：本部分共 5 題，請於聽到播出的一段對話及一個相關的問題之後，從以下各題之 A、B、C、D 四個選項中，選出一個最適合的回答。每題只播出一次。

1. (A) He's taking off too many clothes on him.
   (B) He's doing too much exercise in one time.
   (C) He's playing online games normally and regularly.
   (D) He's on a diet.

2. (A) About rooms filled with wastes.
   (B) About clothing made of reused materials.
   (C) About ideas proposed by an economist.
   (D) About trends passing through the season.

3. (A) She feels regret for it.
   (B) She feels startled by it.
   (C) She feels pleased with it.
   (D) She feels upset about it.

4. (A) He's going to be optimistic.
   (B) He's going to be mad.
   (C) He's going to be sad.
   (D) He's going to be passive.

5. (A) He'll make another shopping bag for her.
   (B) He'll tear his shopping bag for her.
   (C) He'll get another shopping bag for her.
   (D) He'll seal his shopping bag for her.

閱讀能力測驗

一、詞彙與結構：本部份共5題，每題含1個空格。請從以下各題之A、B、C、D四個選項中，選出最適合題意的字詞。

_____ 1. The topnotch restaurant insists on offering _____ food to its customers.

   (A) processed   (B) organic   (C) artificial   (D) organizing

_____ 2. Recently, many experts _____ that CO_2 emission around the globe is over the limit.

   (A) to warn   (B) will warn   (C) had warned   (D) have warned

_____ 3. There is always _____ daylight used for plant growth at night in the green house.

   (A) resolvable   (B) passing   (C) artificial   (D) organic

_____ 4. The lonely old man stood beside the sea, _____ his eyes _____ with tears.

   (A) with; filled   (B) for; filling   (C) by; to fill   (D) into; fill

_____ 5. Every building should be built up for requirement of _____.

   (A) industry   (B) electricity   (C) accessory   (D) sustainability

二、段落填空：本部份共5題，分別為以下段落中的5個空格。請從以下各題之A、B、C、D四個選項中，選出最適合題意的字詞。

The Irish rock star Bono, lead singer in the pop group U2, has spoken out against ___6___ in the Third World and has called on the governments of wealthy countries to do more to help the world's poor. His wife, Ali Hewson, ___7___ he met at school when they were both teenagers, shares his passion for helping people.

___8___ waiting for governments, she believes in acting on her own. She is convinced that the best way to help people in poor countries is not by giving them money, but by offering them jobs ___9___ they can earn money for themselves while still maintaining their pride. As a result, she ___10___ the fashion company EDUN which operates factories in several poor countries in Africa and South America.

_____ 6. (A) infinity   (B) faculty   (C) poverty   (D) gravity
_____ 7. (A) that   (B) whom   (C) what   (D) which
_____ 8. (A) Because of   (B) In view of   (C) In spite of   (D) Instead of

9. (A) so that   (B) so as   (C) such as   (D) such that

10. (A) found   (B) founded   (C) bound   (D) bounded

三、閱讀理解：本部分共5題，包含一段短文，後有5個相關問題。請從以下各題之A、B、C、D四個選項中，選出最適合題意的答案。

For many people around the world, the lifestyle of environmental protection has become an important decision point. Most of today's environmental problems are caused by we people, but they can also be fixed by us.

Fossil fuels are energy sources that are collected from underground, such as oil, natural gas, and coal. They are burned mainly to create heat and electricity. However, burning them brings serious air pollution. Fossil fuels are non-renewable resources. One day they will run out, and human beings will be left without fuel and power.

Air pollution is the major cause of the greenhouse effect. Certain gases, called greenhouse gases, gather in the air, trapping the sun's heat and radiation in earth's atmosphere. This causes the worldwide temperature to rise over time and then leads to the global warming. The global warming is mostly responsible for melting ice in the North Pole, making water levels soar, and then, in as little as 50 years, making cities near oceans sink underwater.

Presently, there are plans to create and use clean, renewable power, usually called "green" energy. It includes sources such as solar, wind, and hydroelectric power. There is even research to turn garbage into power.

11. What is the passage mainly about?

    (A) An old energy to be stolen.

    (B) A good lifestyle to be learned.

    (C) An environmental problem to be solved.

    (D) A research to be conducted.

12. How does the author think of the problem of human energy consumption?

    (A) It is a vital issue.   (B) It is a cliché.

    (C) It is a pie in the sky.   (D) It is a piece of cake.

_____ 13. Which of the following is NOT included as a possible renewable energy source?

(A) Trash.   (B) The sun.   (C) Wind.   (D) Grass.

_____ 14. Which of the following is NOT mentioned as a problem of burning fossil fuels?

(A) The greenhouse effect.   (B) Too many sites for burning garbage.

(C) Air pollution.   (D) Running out of power.

_____ 15. What is the most serious effect the global warming will cause on earth?

(A) Earth's atmosphere will fall.

(B) Cities at the coast will sink.

(C) The North Pole ice will renew.

(D) Problems in human society will resolve.

寫作能力測驗

一、 中譯英：請將下列的一段中文翻譯成通順、達意且前後連貫的英文。

> 近年來，帶有關懷地球理念的「樂活」(LOHAS) 一直被討論。許多人已經加入樂活一族，食用有機食物，使用回收器具，盡量節省能源，而且努力倡導「樂活」。

二、 英文作文：請依以下的提示寫一篇英文作文，長度約120字(8至12個句子)。(評分重點包括內容、組織、文法、用字、標點、大小寫)。

> 提示：多年來，台灣各地街頭補習班 (cram schools) 林立。請就你親身補習過的經驗或是你所得到的資訊，討論學生到補習班補習的原因。

聽力測驗

64 簡短對話：本部分共 5 題，請於聽到播出的一段對話及一個相關的問題之後，從以下各題之 A、B、C、D 四個選項中，選出一個最適合的回答。每題只播出一次。

1. (A) She's very busy with entertainment.

   (B) She's so busy entertaining her friends.

   (C) She's not permitted for entertainment by the police.

   (D) She's not supposed to have time for entertainment.

2. (A) Impolite behaviors will ruin one's image.

   (B) Inconsiderate words can hurt people's feelings.

   (C) Important terms should remain a secret.

   (D) Indirect questions can confuse listeners.

3. (A) It should be a hidden problem.

   (B) It should be a huge mistake.

   (C) It should be a correct usage.

   (D) It should be a wrong choice.

4. (A) She learns the term in films.

   (B) She hears the term in her hometown.

   (C) She learns the term in America.

   (D) She reads the term in books.

5. (A) It's important to look over.

   (B) It's unnecessary to worry about.

   (C) It's convenient to skip over.

   (D) It's difficult to pay off.

閱讀能力測驗

一、詞彙與結構：本部份共5題，每題含1個空格。請從以下各題之A、B、C、D四個選項中，選出最適合題意的字詞。

_____ 1. The famous celebrity couple is getting divorced because the differences between them haven't been _____ for years.

(A) commented　　(B) overused　　(C) resolved　　(D) blurred

_____ 2. The air crash badly occurred to _____ an extent _____ no one could survive.

(A) so; as　　(B) so; that　　(C) such; as　　(D) such; that

_____ 3. The _____ of senior citizens should be valued, for they've been through thick and thin.

(A) experiences　　(B) conditions　　(C) expressions　　(D) commercials

_____ 4. If you _____ for this exam earlier, you _____ much better than now.

(A) had prepared; should perform　　(B) prepared; would perform
(C) have prepared; can perform　　(D) are preparing; may perform

_____ 5. Many celebrities choose to _____ fame and wealth for their family and friends.

(A) result　　(B) substitute　　(C) challenge　　(D) remind

二、段落填空：本部份共5題，分別為以下段落中的5個空格。請從以下各題之A、B、C、D四個選項中，選出最適合題意的字詞。

I need your help!

Everybody seems ___6___ I am weird. My mother even tells me that I'm really strange, because the way I talk makes people uncomfortable. I don't agree with her, but I think she's right. I always feel I'm speaking a different language.

___7___, I was walking down the street yesterday when a man stole my purse. Luckily, the police caught him. Yet when we got to the police station, everyone ___8___ me. When they asked if he was the thief, I told them he was morally challenged. For their records, they asked if he was bald and I told them he was comb-free. ___9___, the police just let him go because they said I didn't give enough ___10___.

I was just trying to be polite and politically correct. What did I do wrong?

_____ 6. (A) think　　(B) to think　　(C) thinking　　(D) thought

7. (A) Later on   (B) By far   (C) For example   (D) Not yet

8. (A) got mad at   (B) cried out at   (C) ran out of   (D) made use of

9. (A) By the way   (B) In the end   (C) To the best   (D) Across the border

10. (A) stereotype   (B) question   (C) audience   (D) evidence

三、閱讀理解：本部分共5題，包含一段短文，後有5個相關問題。請從以下各題之A、B、C、D四個選項中，選出最適合題意的答案。

In the age of political correctness, companies are removing traditional stereotypes and images from advertising. However, while different races have been treated with more respect in recent years, women seem to have been left behind in the PC movement. Nowhere is this more obvious than in beer commercials.

Around the world, beer companies continue to exploit female sexuality. Bars and stores in nearly every country have posters of women in swimsuits holding their beer of choice. The German beer, St. Pauli Girl, features the image of a servant girl on the bottle. A video from a beer festival in Kenting, Taiwan, now popular on the Internet, shows thinly dressed young women dancing on stage.

Unfortunately, it is not just women's sexuality that is still being exploited in beer commercials. A recent Italian ad pokes fun at the stereotypical idea that women are bad drivers. A group of female lawyers, however, do not see the humor. They are suing the beer company for being sexist and discriminatory.

It is unclear why women have been largely ignored by beer companies in the PC movement. Whatever the cause may be, it is important that we as a society give thought to this issue.

11. What is the passage mainly about?

    (A) Beer commercial of PC.   (B) Lawyers opposite to PC.

    (C) Females excluded from PC.   (D) Drivers in favor of PC.

12. In what way do the beer companies exploit women's images?

    (A) By telling lies to females.   (B) By mistaking females for males.

    (C) By giving surprises to females.   (D) By misusing female sexuality.

13. How does the group of female lawyers think of the Italian ad?

    (A) They thought it humorous.   (B) They thought it expensive.

    (C) They thought it discriminatory.   (D) They thought it important.

14. What image of females does the author imply that males probably prefer?

(A) Barely dressed women.　　(B) Excellent drivers.

(C) Angry lawyers.　　(D) Desperate housewives.

15. What is the author's attitude toward the stereotypical advertising against females?

(A) It needs to be done more.　　(B) It needs to be thought over.

(C) It takes time to be accepted.　　(D) It takes much effort to finish.

寫作能力測驗

一、中譯英：請將下列的一段中文翻譯成通順、達意且前後連貫的英文。

　　使用政治正確語言是為了尊重其他人與我們之間的差異。不論是針對他人的外在特徵或是其社會地位，我們都應該為他人的感覺著想，而注意自己的措詞。

二、英文作文：請依以下的提示寫一篇英文作文，長度約120字(8至12個句子)。(評分重點包括內容、組織、文法、用字、標點、大小寫)。

提示：近幾年來，全球暖化 (global warming) 的現象一直是世人共同關注的議題。請就你所得到的資訊，討論全球暖化對於自然環境和人類文明可能造成的後果。

WORD BANK FOR READINGS

Unit 1

 CORE READING (page 18)

1. fabulous [ˈfæbjələs] *adj.* 極好的
2. online [ˈɑnˌlaɪn] *adj.* (電腦) 連線的
3. in contrast 相反地
4. pace [pes] *n.* 步調;速度
5. romance [roˈmæns] *n.* 戀情
6. physical [ˈfɪzɪkl̩] *adj.* 身體的
7. intimacy [ˈɪntəməsɪ] *n.* 親密
8. Korea [ˈkorɪˌɑ] *n.* 韓國
9. outsider [autˈsaɪdɚ] *n.* 外人;局外人
10. uneasy [ʌnˈizɪ] *adj.* 不自在的
11. complicated [ˈkɑmpləˌketɪd] *adj.* 複雜的
12. bond [bɑnd] *n.* 聯繫;關係
13. soften [ˈsɔfən] *v.* 使…軟化;使…溫和

 EXTENDED READING I (page 20)

1. bloom [blum] *v.* 開花,花盛開
2. gaze [gez] *v.* 凝視
3. affection [əˈfɛkʃən] *n.* 情感
4. refer [rɪˈfɝ] *v.* 有關係;指 (的是)
5. illegal [ɪˈligl̩] *adj.* 不合法的
6. inappropriate [ˌɪnəˈpropriɪt] *adj.* 不適當的
7. supervise [ˌsupɚˈvaɪz] *v.* 監督
8. hood [hud] *n.* (獵鷹的) 頭罩
9. falcon [ˈfɔlkən] *n.* 獵鷹
10. accompany [əˈkʌmpənɪ] *v.* 陪同;伴隨
11. virtue [ˈvɝtʃu] *n.* 德行
12. godfather [ˈgɑdˌfɑðɚ] *n.* 教父
13. ruin [ˈruɪn] *v.* 破壞

 EXTENDED READING II (page 22)

1. utter [ˈʌtɚ] *v.* 說出;發出 (聲音)
2. awkward [ˈɔkwɚd] *adj.* 尷尬的
3. impatiently [ɪmˈpeʃəntlɪ] *adv.* 沒耐心地

4. participant [pɑrˈtɪsəpənt] *n.* 參與者
5. scorecard [ˈskorˌkɑrd] *n.* 記分板
6. assign [əˈsaɪn] *v.* 分配
7. rotate [ˈrotet] *v.* 交替,輪換
8. Tokyo [ˈtokɪˌo] *n.* 東京 (日本首都)
9. sponsor [ˈspɑnsɚ] *v.* 資助
10. populated [ˈpɑpjəˌletɪd] *adj.* 人口眾多的
11. embarrassment [ɪmˈbærəsmənt] *n.* 尷尬
12. discomfort [dɪsˈkʌmfɚt] *n.* 不自在

Unit 2

 CORE READING (page 32)

1. tough [tʌf] *adj.* 堅定的,強悍的
2. armed [ɑrmd] *adj.* 武裝的
3. battlefield [ˈbætl̩ˌfild] *n.* 戰場
4. participation [pɚˌtɪsəˌpeʃən] *n.* 參與
5. Asia [ˈeʒə] *n.* 亞洲
6. leading [ˈlidɪŋ] *adj.* 領先的
7. status [ˈstetəs] *n.* 地位

 EXTENDED READING I (page 34)

1. Norway [ˈnɔrwe] *n.* 挪威
2. parental [pəˈrɛntl̩] *adj.* 父母的
3. Portugal [ˈportʃəgl̩] *n.* 葡萄牙
4. Guatemala [ˌgwɑtəˈmɑlə] *n.* 瓜地馬拉
5. sleepless [ˈsliplɪs] *adj.* 不睡覺的;不休息的

 EXTENDED READING II (page 36)

1. fearless [ˈfɪrlɪs] *adj.* 無懼的
2. Viking [ˈvaɪkɪŋ] *n.* 維京人 (中世紀的北歐海盜)
3. dominate [ˈdɑməˌnet] *v.* 支配,佔最大影響力
4. nevertheless [ˌnɛvɚðəˈlɛs] *adv.* 然而
5. numerous [ˈnjumərəs] *adj.* 很多的
6. inspirational [ˌɪnspəˈreʃənl̩] *adj.* 激勵人心的
7. superpower [ˌsupɚˈpauɚ] *n.* 超級強國

8. confront [kən`frʌnt] v. 對抗

9. British [`brɪtɪʃ] adj. 英國的

10. saint [sent] n. 聖人

11. contribution [ˌkɑntrə`bjuʃən] n. 貢獻

12. Ireland [`aɪrlənd] n. 愛爾蘭

13. presidency [`prɛzədənsɪ] n. 總統職位

14. devoted [dɪ`votɪd] v. 奉獻 (時間)

15. Africa [`æfrɪkə] n. 非洲

16. remarkable [rɪ`mɑrkəbḷ] adj. 值得注意的，引人注目的

17. chancellor [`tʃænsələ˞] n. (德國、奧地利) 總理

18. Argentina [ˌɑrdʒən`tinə] n. 阿根延

19. senator [`sɛnətə˞] n. 參議員

20. landslide [`lænd,slaɪd] n. (選舉的) 壓倒性勝利

Unit 3

🎧71 CORE READING   (page 46)

1. handsome [`hænsəm] n. (數量) 可觀的

2. candidate [`kændə,det] n. 候選人

3. initiate [ɪ`nɪʃɪ,et] v. 開始

4. skateboard [`sket,bord] n. 滑板

5. exotic [ɪg`zɑtɪk] adj. 奇特的

6. underpants [`ʌndə˞,pænts] n. pl. 內衣褲

7. nowadays [`nauə,dez] adv. 現今

8. Internet surfer   網路漫游者

9. potential [pə`tɛnʃəl] adj. 潛在的，可能的

10. globe [glob] n. 地球；世界

11. billionaire [ˌbɪljən`ɛr] n. 億萬富翁

🎧72 EXTENDED READING I   (page 48)

1. tuna [`tunə] n. 鮪魚

2. moon cake   月餅

3. access [`æksɛs] n. 接近的辦法

4. confidence [ˌkɑnfə`dæn] n. 信心

5. career [kə`rɪr] n. 生涯；事業

6. statistics [stə`tɪstɪk] n. (pl.) 統計數字

7. conference [`kɑnfərəns] n. 會議

8. otoro [ɔ`tɔlɔ] n. 黑鮪魚前腹肉

9. frozen [`frozṇ] adj. 冷凍的

10. meantime [`min,taɪm] adv. 同時間

11. inclined [ɪn`klaɪnd] adj. 傾向於；易於

12. training [`trenɪŋ] n. 訓練

13. inspire [ɪn`spaɪr] v. 激勵

14. option [`ɑpʃən] n. 選擇

🎧73 EXTENDED READING II   (page 50)

1. imply [ɪm`plaɪ] v. 意指；暗示

2. conventional [kən`vɛnʃənḷ] adj. 慣例的；傳統的

3. broker [`brokə˞] n. 仲介人；股票經紀人

4. challenging [`tʃælɪndʒɪn] adj. 具有挑戰性的

5. distraction [dɪ`strækʃən] n. 分心的事物，娛樂

6. sneak [snik] v. 偷偷的行動、進出

7. vital [`vaɪtḷ] adj. 極為重要的

8. deadline [`dɛd,laɪn] n. 截止日期

9. unpleased [ˌʌn`plizd] adj. 不高興的

10. irregular [ɪ`rɛgjələ˞] adj. 無規律的

11. profitable [`prɑfɪtəbḷ] adj. 有利的，賺錢的

Unit 4

🎧74 CORE READING   (page 60)

1. profile [`profaɪl] n. 人物介紹，簡介

2. nightmare [`naɪt,mɛr] n. 夢魘

3. annoying [ə`nɔɪɪŋ] adj. 惱人的

4. photo-taker [`foto`tekə˞] n. 攝影者

5. incident [`ɪnsədent] n. 偶發事件

6. helicopter [`hɛlɪ,kɑptə˞] n. 直升機

7. sue [su] v. 控告

8. invade [ɪn`ved] v. 侵犯

9. privacy [`praɪvəsɪ] n. 隱私

10. pursuit [pə˞`sut] n. 追蹤；追擊

11. crazed [krezd] *adj.* 瘋狂的

12. Paris [ˋpærɪs] *n.* 巴黎 (法國首都)

13. opening night　首場演出

14. buzz [bʌz] *n.* 小道消息

(75) EXTENDED READING I　(page 62)

1. witness [ˋwɪtnɪs] *v.* 目擊

2. catchy [ˋkætʃɪ] *adj.* 吸引人的

3. stirring [ˋstɝɪŋ] *adj.* 激動人心的

4. embarrassing [ɪmˋbærəsɪŋ] *adj.* 使人難堪的

5. sell like hot cakes　銷路好，很暢銷

6. Britain [ˋbrɪtn̩] *n.* 英國

7. The National Enquirer　國家詢問報 (美國八卦報紙)

8. presentation [͵prɛzn̩ˋteʃən] *n.* 介紹，陳述

9. criticism [ˋkrɪtə͵sɪzəm] *n.* 批評；評論

10. tailgate [ˋtel͵get] *v.* (口語) 緊隨前車行駛

11. tragedy [ˋtrædʒədɪ] *n.* 悲劇事件

12. tall tale　誇大的故事

13. deserve [dɪˋzɝv] *v.* 應得

14. distorted [dɪsˋtɔrtɪd] *adj.* 扭曲的

(76) EXTENDED READING II　(page 64)

1. totally [ˋtotl̩ɪ] *adv.* 完全地

2. desperately [ˋdɛspərɪtlɪ] *adv.* 極度地

3. premier [ˋprimɪɚ] *n.* 首映

4. hazard [ˋhæzɚd] *n.* 危險因素，危險之源

5. rage [redʒ] *n.* 憤怒

6. bodyguard [ˋbɑdɪ͵gɑrd] *n.* 保鑣

7. thrill [θrɪl] *n.* 令人感到刺激的樂趣

Unit 5

(77) CORE READING　(page 74)

1. structural [ˋstrʌktʃərəl] *adj.* 建築上的，結構的

2. instillation [͵ɪnstɪˋleʃən] *n.* 灌輸

3. orderly [ˋɔrdɚlɪ] *adj.* 有秩序的

4. India [ˋɪndɪə] *n.* 印度

5. disorderly [dɪsˋɔrdɚlɪ] *adj.* 無秩序的

6. construct [kənˋstrʌkt] *v.* 建構

(78) EXTENDED READING I　(page 76)

1. afar [əˋfɑr] *adv.* 遙遠地

2. shocking [ˋʃɑkɪŋ] *adj.* 令人震驚的

3. philosopher [fəˋlɑsəfɚ] *n.* 哲學家

4. castrate [ˋkæstret] *v.* 閹割

5. cemetery [ˋsɛmə͵tɛrɪ] *n.* 墓地

6. tomb [tum] *n.* 墳墓

(79) EXTENDED READING II　(page 78)

1. holistic [hoˋlɪstɪk] *adj.* 全觀的

2. Aconcagua [͵ækɔŋˋkɑgwə] *n.* 阿空加瓜山 (西半球最高峰)

3. backpack [ˋbæk͵pæk] *n.* 背包

4. Celsius [ˋsɛlsɪəs] *n.* 攝氏

5. innovative [ˋɪnə͵vetɪv] *adj.* 創新的

6. alternative [ɔlˋtɝnətɪv] *adj.* 既有體制之外的

7. schooling [ˋskulɪŋ] *n.* 學校教育

8. creativity [͵krieˋtɪvətɪ] *n.* 創造力

9. elementary [͵ɛləˋmɛntərɪ] *adj.* 初級的，基礎的

10. forerunner [forˋrʌnɚ] *n.* 先驅

11. founder [ˋfaʊndɚ] *n.* 創立者

12. convinced [kənˋvɪnst] *adj.* 確信的

13. attendance [əˋtɛndəns] *n.* 出席

14. voluntary [ˋvɑlən͵tɛrɪ] *adj.* 自願的

15. adjust [əˋdʒʌst] *v.* 使適應於

16. eventually [ɪˋvɛntʃʊlɪ] *adv.* 最終

17. conquer [ˋkɑŋkɚ] *v.* 征服

18. coexist [͵koɪgˋzɪst] *v.* 共存

Unit 6

(80) CORE READING (page 88)

1. harshly [`harʃlɪ] *adv.* 粗暴地
2. dangle [`dæŋgl] *v.* 懸吊
3. tortured [`tɔrtʃəd] *adj.* 受盡折磨的
4. inhuman [ɪn`hjumən] *adj.* 殘忍的，無人性的
5. brutally [`brutlɪ] *adv.* 殘酷地
6. monitoring [`manətərɪŋ] *n.* 監視
7. agency [`edʒənsɪ] *n.* 機構
8. declare [dɪ`klɛr] *v.* 宣稱
9. Iran [aɪ`ræn] *n.* 伊朗
10. homosexual [,homə`sɛkʃʊəl] *n.* 同性戀者
11. lash [læʃ] *n.* 鞭打
12. severe [sə`vɪr] *adj.* 嚴酷的
13. imprisonment [ɪm`prɪznmənt] *n.* 監禁
14. allegedly [ə`lɛdʒɪdlɪ] *adv.* 據稱
15. Canada [`kænədə] *n.* 加拿大
16. preference [`prɛfrəns] *n.* 偏好
17. force [fors] *n.* 軍隊
18. discrimination [dɪ,skrɪmə`neʃən] *n.* 歧視
19. partnership [`partnɚ,ʃɪp] *n.* 夥伴關係
20. particularly [pɚ`tɪkjələ·lɪ] *adv.* 尤其
21. Islamic [ɪs`læmɪk] *adj.* 伊斯蘭教的
22. the United Nations (UN) *n.* 聯合國
23. consult [kən`sʌlt] *v.* 商量，協議
24. homophobia [,homə`fobɪə] *n.* 對同性戀者的恐懼

(81) EXTENDED READING I (page 90)

1. banner [`bænɚ] *n.* 旗；橫幅旗
2. annually [`ænjʊəlɪ] *adv.* 一年一次的
3. expand [ɪk`spænd] *v.* 擴大
4. campaign [kæm`pen] *n.* (社會的) 活動、運動
5. mistreat [mɪs`trit] *v.* 不當對待
6. irritate [`ɪrə,tet] *v.* 激怒
7. trigger [`trɪgɚ] *v.* 引發，引起

8. community [kə`mjunətɪ] *n.* (相同關係的) 團體
9. mode [mod] *n.* 模式

(82) EXTENDED READING II (page 92)

1. Halloween [,hælo`in] *n.* 萬聖節前夕
   (10 月 31 日晚上)
2. theme [θim] *n.* 主題
3. legalize [`ligl,aɪz] *v.* 合法化
4. denial [dɪ`naɪəl] *n.* 否認
5. insurance coverage 保險項目 (範圍)
6. spouse [spauz] *n.* 配偶
7. operation [,apə`reʃən] *n.* 手術
8. document [`dakjə,mənt] *n.* 文件
9. Israel [`ɪzrɪəl] *n.* 以色列
10. Mexico [`mɛksɪ,ko] *n.* 墨西哥
11. acknowledge [ək`nalɪdʒ] *v.* 認可
12. Buenos Aires [`bonəs`ɛriz] *n.* 布宜諾艾利斯
    (阿根廷首都)
13. heterosexual [,hɛtərə`sɛkʃʊəl] *adj.* 異性戀的

Unit 7

(83) CORE READING (page 102)

1. blend [blɛnd] *n.* 混合物
2. resolvable [rɪ`zalvəbl] *adj.* 可分解 (溶解) 的
3. detergent [dɪ`tɝdʒənt] *n.* 洗潔劑
4. solar-powered [`solɚ`pauɚd] *adj.* 太陽能發電的
5. hybrid-generated [`haɪbrɪd`dʒɛnə,retɪd] *adj.* 汽電
   共生發電的
6. sustainability [sə,stenə`bɪlɪtɪ] *n.* 永續性
7. estimate [`ɛstə,met] *v.* 估計
8. revenue [`rɛvə,nju] *n.* 收益
9. ingredient [ɪn`gridɪənt] *n.* 成份
10. artificial [,artə`fɪʃəl] *adj.* 人造的
11. compound [kam`paund] *n.* 化合物
12. preferable [`prɛfrəbl] *adj.* 更可取的

13. renovate [ˋrɛnəˏvet] v. 更新

14. renewable [rɪˋnjuəbl] adj. 可再生的

15. hydroelectric [ˏhaɪdroɪˋlɛktrɪk] adj. 水力發電的

 EXTENDED READING I (page 104)

1. runway [ˋrʌnˏwe] n. 伸展台

2. eco [ˋiko] adj. 生態學的

3. glamorous [ˋglæmərəs] adj. 迷人的

4. dazzling [ˋdæzlɪŋ] adj. 閃亮奪目的

5. absolutely [ˋæbsəˏlutlɪ] adv. 絕對地

6. creation [krɪˋeʃən] n. (服裝等的) 新款式

7. front-runner [ˋfrʌntˋrʌnɚ] n. 領先的人

8. trendy [ˋtrɛndɪ] adj. 最新流行的

9. manufacture [ˏmænjəˋfæktʃɚ] v. 製造

10. labor [ˋlebɚ] n. 勞動；努力

11. ironically [aɪˋrɑnɪklɪ] adv. 諷刺地

12. consume [kənˋsum] v. 消耗

13. fad [fæd] n. 流行一時的狂熱

 EXTENDED READING II (page 106)

1. production [prəˋdʌkʃən] n. 生產

2. carbon dioxide (CO_2) 二氧化碳

3. emission [ɪˋmɪʃən] n. 排放

4. cattle shed 牛舍

5. machinery [məˋʃinərɪ] n. 機械

6. refrigerate [rɪˋfrɪdʒəˏret] v. 冷藏

7. farming [ˋfɑrmɪŋ] n. 飼養

8. conserve [kənˋsɝv] v. 節省

9. Swedish [ˋswidɪʃ] n. 瑞典人

10. conduct [kənˋdʌkt] v. 執行

11. vegetarian [ˏvɛdʒəˋtɛrɪən] n. 素食者

Unit 8

 CORE READING (page 116)

1. substitute [ˋsʌbstəˏtjut] v. 代替

2. blur [blɝ] v. 模糊不清

3. critic [ˋkrɪtɪk] n. 批評家

4. overuse [ˏovɚˋjuz] v. 過度使用

5. extent [ɪkˋstɛnt] n. 程度

6. dwarf [dwɔrf] n. 矮子

7. vertically challenged 垂直方向有問題 (「個子矮」的委婉說法)

8. empathy [ˋɛmpəθɪ] n. 同感

 EXTENDED READING I (page 118)

1. shorty [ˋʃɔrtɪ] n. (口語，輕蔑語) 矮個子

2. oldie [ˋoldɪ] n. 老人

3. comment [ˋkɑmɛnt] v. 評論

4. scenery [ˋsinərɪ] n. 景色

 EXTENDED READING II (page 120)

1. toothpaste [ˋtuθˏpest] n. 牙膏

2. correctness [kəˋrɛktnɪs] n. 正確

3. resolve [rɪˋzɑlv] v. 解決

4. herbal medicine 中醫學，藥草醫學

5. gourmet [ˋgʊrme] n. 美食家

6. recipe [ˋrɛsəpɪ] n. 食譜

7. sparkling [ˋspɑrklɪŋ] adj. 閃閃發光的

8. Asian [ˋeʒən] n. 亞洲人

9. shining [ˋʃaɪnɪŋ] adj. 閃耀的

10. advertiser [ˋædvɚˏtaɪzɚ] n. 廣告業者

11. marketing [ˋmɑrkɪtɪŋ] n. 行銷

12. irrational [ɪˋræʃənl] adj. 不理性的

13. consequently [ˏkɑnsəˋkwɛntlɪ] adv. 因此，所以

14. repeatedly [rɪˋpitɪdlɪ] adv. 重複地

15. slogan [ˋslogən] n. 標語，口號

ALL IN READING book one、book two

全方位英文閱讀
余光雄 編著

本書題材以「文化比較」為主軸,將內容延伸至聽、說、讀、寫四大層面上:

1. 本書以增進學生英文閱讀和理解能力為目標。課文選自國外教材,主題生活化,讀來活潑有趣。
2. 每課均有聽、說、讀、寫四大單元,讓學生均衡發展英文四大能力。
3. 版面設計採用豐富多元的照片和插圖,教學使用更活潑;標題依照四大能力分類設計,功能分類一目了然。
4. 本書並附有教師手冊、朗讀光碟及電子教學投影片。

HOSPITALITY ENGLISH AND CONVERSATION

餐旅英文與會話 I〜IV
黃招憲、David Walter Goodman 編著

1. 本書目標為培養學生簡單英文會話能力,因應其工作基本需求。
2. 共分12課,每課針對會話主題及溝通功能 (functions) 所設計,包括 Getting Started (暖身活動)、Conversations (對話)、Useful Expressions (實用語)、Oral Practice (口語練習) 和 Listening Practice (聽力練習) 等單元,幫助學生建立穩固的會話基礎。
3. 附有教師手冊及由專業外籍人士所錄製的朗讀光碟,以讓學生熟悉 native speaker 的發音和語調。

ENJOY READING 悅讀50   王隆興 編著

1. 精選50篇多元主題的文章，篇篇妙筆生花，精彩好讀。
2. 命題方向符合各類大考趨勢，讓您熟能生巧，輕取高分。
3. 特聘優質外籍作者親撰文章，語法用字純正道地。
4. 文章程度符合大考中心公佈之單字表中4000字的範圍，難度適中。
5. 本書備有解析本。

英語口語練習 I～VI   蔡玟玲、吳企方 編著

1. 本書融合聽、說、讀、寫四個部份，以溝通式教學（communicative approach）為導向。
2. 就功能而言，每課分成兩個階段：第一階段包括閱讀、重要單字等的練習活動；第二階段主要功能為增進聽力或口語表達能力，如代換練習、角色扮演等。
3. 全書編寫以日常生活英語會話為主軸，除適合課堂教學外，亦適合自修。
4. 本書備有教師手冊。

英文寫作練習 I～IV   黃素月 編著

本套書適合學習英文多年，但仍欠缺完整寫作訓練的讀者。在教學設計上，本書運用多種教學理論，作者群教學經驗豐富，妥善巧妙地將理論與實際教學經驗連結，是國內少見的本土版完整英文寫作教材。

本套書並附有豐富的範文及例句。書中所選範文，皆與青少年生活、重要時事以及其他國家的有趣文化和社會現象息息相關。寫作活動的安排由淺入深，每個活動皆標示難易度，可配合讀者的程度。本套書並備有教師手冊及解答本。

實用英文文法   馬洵、劉紅英、郭立穎 編著，龔慧懿 編審

1. 文字說明深入淺出、讓您輕鬆學習。
2. 用字簡明精確、易懂易記，絕不讓您讀得「霧煞煞」。
3. 以圖表方式歸納、條列文法重點，讓您對文法規則一目了然。
4. 書中文法搭配上千條例句，情境兼具普遍性和專業性，並附有中文翻譯，便於自學。

國家圖書館出版品預行編目資料

HEAD START II / 車蓓群主編;李雪佛編著.－－
初版一刷.－－臺北市：三民，2008
冊；　公分

ISBN 978–957–14–4824–4　(第一冊：平裝)
ISBN 978–957–14–5027–8　(第二冊：平裝)
1. 英語 2. 讀本

805.18　　　　　　　　　　　　96014959

© **HEAD　START　II**

主　　　編	車蓓群 (Patricia Che)
編 著 者	李雪佛
責任編輯	許嘉諾
版面設計	蔡季吟
插畫設計	王孟婷　吳　騏　林家蓁
發 行 人	劉振強
著作財產權人	三民書局股份有限公司
發 行 所	三民書局股份有限公司
	地址　臺北市復興北路386號
	電話　(02)25006600
	郵撥帳號　0009998–5
門 市 部	(復北店) 臺北市復興北路386號
	(重南店) 臺北市重慶南路一段61號
出版日期	初版一刷　2008年3月
編　　號	S 807110

行政院新聞局登記證局版臺業字第○二○○號

有著作權・不准侵害

ISBN　978–957–14–5027–8　(第二冊：平裝)